Then as if fate stepped in, her eyes snagged on the lower half of a man descending from a pretty spiral staircase that she'd not noticed earlier.

Even if men weren't a priority for Olivia, a little blip of pleasure registered on her radar. Black-trousers-covered legs that went all the way up—and up—the fabric lovingly clasped around muscled thighs, a firm, rounded, super-hero-in-tights butt. Nice.

A girl deserved a little lust blip every now and then and this blip was brightening by the second.

His gaze met hers as if she'd summoned him to look her way. And he didn't look pleased about that. His eyebrows lowered, his mouth firmed and a muscle clenched in his jaw.

Steely black eyes with the power to tempt. To persuade. A shiver rippled down her spine. The power to take her will and flex it between his long slender fingers like so much overcooked spaghetti.

And Olivia felt hot, like she did when standing on the steaming deck of her yacht on a mid-summer's day in Barbados. In the eye of a tropical storm even, because her usually strong sea legs were wobbly.

She was still looking at him and he was still looking at her and she swore she saw him mouth, 'Trouble'.

Praise for Anne Oliver

'This sweet and sexy story has engaging characters that will captivate readers from the very first page.'
—*RT Book Reviews* on
There's Something About a Rebel

'Quick paced, this story has a sensitive hero that readers will easily fall in love with.'
—*RT Book Reviews* on *Her Not-So-Secret Diary*

'This attraction-at-first-sight story has just the right blend of adventure, passion and heartfelt emotion to make you want to spend time with this terrific twosome.'
—*RT Book Reviews* on *Hot Boss, Wicked Nights*

MISTLETOE
NOT REQUIRED

BY
ANNE OLIVER

First published in Great Britain 2013
by Mills & Boon, an imprint of Harlequin (UK) Limited,
Harlequin (UK) Limited, Eton House, 18-24 Paradise Road,
Richmond, Surrey TW9 1SR

© Anne Oliver 2013

ISBN: 978 0 263 91070 4

Harlequin (UK) policy is to use papers that are natural, renewable and recyclable products and made from wood grown in sustainable forests. The logging and manufacturing processes conform to the legal environmental regulations of the country of origin.

Printed and bound in Spain
by Blackprint CPI, Barcelona

Anne Oliver was born in Adelaide, South Australia, with its beautiful hills, beaches and easy lifestyle. She's never left.

An avid reader of romance, Anne began creating her own paranormal and time travel adventures in 1998, before turning to contemporary romance. Then it happened— she was accepted by Mills & Boon in December 2005. Almost as exciting, her first two published novels won the Romance Writers of Australia's Romantic Book of the Year for 2007 and 2008. So, after nearly thirty years of yard duties and staff meetings, she gave up teaching to do what she loves most—writing full time.

Other interests include animal welfare and conservation, quilting, astronomy, all things Scottish, and eating anything she doesn't have to cook. She's travelled to Papua New Guinea, the west coast of America, Hong Kong, Malaysia, the UK and Holland.

Sharing her characters' journeys with readers all over the world is a privilege and a dream come true. You can visit her website at www.anne-oliver.com.

This book is dedicated to anyone whose lives have been touched by breast cancer—mums, daughters, sisters, aunts, grandmothers. And the men who support them. That's pretty much everyone really.

With thanks to Wendy for making my time in beautiful Tasmania even more enjoyable.

With thanks to my editor, Suzanne Clarke, for putting in the hard work on my hero.

CHAPTER ONE

OLIVIA WISHART SLICKED ruby gloss on her lips, then checked her strapless cocktail dress in the mirror and frowned. 'Red lips, red dress, red hair.' She reached for her standby little black dress. 'I don't care if everyone's decked to the halls in Christmas finery, it's—'

'Lovely, but not for tonight.' Her best friend, Breanna Black, whipped the garment from her hand. 'And not another word—you look sensational.' She eyed the cleavage on display and nodded. 'Wise choice—men will look.'

'So long as they listen.' Olivia wasn't a fancy dress fan but the opportunity to talk up her charity to her fellow competitors in this year's Sydney to Hobart Yacht Race was too good to pass up. And a little flesh never failed to get attention.

'Try to remember, it *is* Christmas.' Brie shimmied into a short mulberry all-in-one playsuit with a fur-trim neckline then tossed Olivia a white feather boa. 'Here. It'll put you in the mood.'

Olivia's lips twitched as she slung the silky feathers around her neck. 'I assume you're referring to the *festive* mood.'

'That'd be a start,' Brie suggested, brightly.

Raising the Pink Snowflake Foundation's profile was the reason for Olivia's entry into the race. Being invited by yachting royalty to celebrate the festive season at the mega-million-dollar mansion overlooking Sydney Harbour was a bonus, but anything else...well, it wasn't going to happen.

Brie unravelled a luscious strand of silver tinsel. 'You're sure you don't mind if Jett shares our suite?' she asked for the umpteenth time.

'This mysterious brother you've managed to keep out of the way for— How long's it been?' Stepping into red stiletto sandals, Olivia reassured her, 'I told you I don't mind. I'm interested to meet him actually.'

Brie paused in her task of twisting the tinsel into her hair. '*Half*-brother. And it's a slow, fraught process. Jett's a hard guy to get to know. I'm not sure he even likes me.'

Olivia smiled. 'What's not to like? And he accepted your invitation, didn't he?'

'Only because his initial plans fell through.'

'You don't know that for sure.' But Olivia was pretty sure *she* did. Classic irresponsible, egocentric male behaviour. Yes, she was absolutely interested to meet him, even if it was only to make certain he knew how much he meant to Brie.

Sighing, Brie flipped her reef of long black hair over her shoulder. 'It makes me feel bad that I'm going away for New Year's Eve now, but he told me not to alter my plans on his account.'

'And why should you? If you're right about *his* plans, he's the one who changed his mind and decided to come at the last minute.'

It was obvious Brie cared but apparently the lost sibling she'd spent three years looking for didn't give a toss. Even though they were as close as sisters, Olivia had decided it was a sensitive issue and none of her business unless Brie opened up to her. 'When's his flight due in?'

'Any time. I'll let the front desk know to expect him before I leave—' Brie's mobile buzzed and she checked caller ID. 'That's him now. Hi, Jett...'

Olivia saw her friend's smile fade, and the temptation to snatch the phone and give him a piece of her mind was overwhelming. She had to turn away. *None of your business, remember.*

'Oh… Uh-huh. Okay. You've got the party's address? I'll meet you there. Text me when you're here,' Olivia heard her say before she disconnected. 'His flight's been delayed. Christmas rush; he hasn't even left Melbourne yet.' She flicked through the contacts on her phone, her smile returning. 'Which gives *me* a spare couple of hours to meet the *Horizon Three*'s sexy skipper for a drink downstairs at the bar after all.'

'Good for you,' Olivia enthused, reserving judgement on Jett—for now. She slipped a wad of business cards into her evening purse, handing one to Brie. 'Give him this and highlight our cause. And just remember, sexy skipper or not, he's the enemy come Boxing Day.'

Brie nodded, mobile attached to her ear, obviously waiting for Mr Sexy Skipper to pick up. 'Don't get smashed or pick up any strange men before I get there.'

As if. Olivia preferred to wake up with a clear head and no regrets. Brie, not so much. Differences aside, they made a good team, trusted and looked out for each other. She flipped the end of the boa over her shoulder. 'I promise not to get smashed.'

'And…?'

'Hey, it's a party for yachties, there'll be men. And I don't care if they're strange so long as they're rich and I can persuade them to part with large sums of money. It's Christmas Eve and I'm hopeful.'

'Good luck, then, and be careful, okay? Hi, Liam…' Brie's voice instantly switched to smooth sensuality.

'Back at you,' Olivia murmured as she slipped out of their

suite and headed downstairs to summon the driver they'd
organised exclusively for the entire evening.

As the chauffeured vehicle made its way across the
bridge, Olivia's thoughts weren't so much on the harbour's
glittering light show, but on the session she'd attended as
a mandatory part of the genetics testing she'd undergone
last week.

Her counsellor had said it could take weeks before she
had the results. A chill ran deep through her bones. She'd
never have taken the test if her mother hadn't made her
promise to have it before her twenty-sixth birthday—the
age her maternal grandmother had been when she'd been
diagnosed with breast cancer.

So she'd done it. Two months late, but she'd done it. Ful-
filled her mother's death-bed request. She'd been so busy,
it had been easy to push aside her own needs—or as Brie
had said, to bury her head in the sand—but now it was real
and she could no longer deny the probability that she'd in-
herited the same mutant gene.

She wrapped her boa tighter around her shoulders. At
least the result, whatever the verdict, would bring relief from
the uncertainty she'd lived with as long as she could remember. And she'd deal with it in her own way—she had control of that at least.

Until then she refused to think about it. It was Christmas,
she had a yacht race to win, a charity to run.

A life to live.

He was late but Jett Davies skirted the massive gold Christmas tree dominating the black marble foyer as he made his
way up yet another sweeping staircase. The third level was
an outdoor entertainment area and he caught a waft of briny
harbour and freshly mown grass. Winking party lights cast
a muted kaleidoscopic blush over the elite guests wearing

anything and everything from a token nod to the festive season to the full Christmas get-up.

The guest list included the Who's Who of the yachting world from all over the globe, along with their glammed-up wives, lovers and/or mistresses. Seemed anyone with money to throw at Australia's prestigious Sydney to Hobart, one of the world's top and most difficult off-shore yacht races, was partaking of the evening's merrymaking.

A force-field of inquisitive eyes found him as he took a beer from a circulating waiter's tray. Eyes dead ahead, he cut straight to an antique spiral staircase he'd spotted in the corner. He hoped its steep and winding steps would discourage stiletto-heeled females from venturing up. He wasn't looking for an available woman. He was looking for his sister. Or had been until she'd texted him ten minutes ago to say she'd been caught up. Car problems, she'd told him—she'd let him know when she was on her way.

The stairs opened up onto a small viewing platform above the main outdoor entertainment area. Deserted—the way he liked it. Leaning on the rail, he watched the ferries track across the twinkling harbour.

Car problems. Breanna. He didn't know her well but he knew her well enough—there *was* no car and a man was definitely involved. He chugged back on his beer. Perhaps they had more in common than he'd thought.

The band below fired off a set of rocking Christmas tunes and his head throbbed. He didn't do the festive season—all that Kris Kringle nonsense, mistletoe madness and nostalgia.

So why had he agreed with Breanna's suggestion to meet her here instead of the hotel bar? Or *them* as it happened, because Breanna was sharing the suite with a girlfriend. Which had him wondering about the wearer of the strawberry lace panties and matching D-cups hanging over the shower rosette in the second bathroom...

Don't even think about it. He shook trouble away, checked the time. *Ten more minutes, Breanna, and I'm gone.*

Guests were starting to leave when Olivia finally found a moment alone and a semi-secluded spot to sit. She sucked on the straw of her Christmas Jones cocktail—her first alcoholic beverage for the evening—and leaned towards the balcony watching the incandescent candles amongst the garden shrubbery.

Hurry up, Brie.

She'd networked all evening to promote Snowflake and was delighted with the responses and promises for donations. But she and her crew had just come off five days' intensive training on the harbour, her feet were killing her and she was ready for some shut-eye.

Except Brie wasn't answering her phone—but she'd texted a winky face.

Did that mean she'd forgotten their arrangement to be there for each other at the end of the evening or what? Pushing up from her plastic party chair, she considered texting a response to say she was leaving but they'd made a promise to watch out for each other years ago and that had never changed.

Then, as if fate stepped in, her eyes snagged on the lower half of a man descending a pretty spiral staircase that she'd not noticed earlier. Even if men weren't a priority for Olivia, a little blip of pleasure registered on her radar. Black trousers covered legs that went all the way up—and up—the fabric lovingly clasped around muscled thighs, a firm, rounded, superhero-in-tights butt. Nice. A girl deserved a little lust blip every now and then and this blip was brightening by the second.

He reached the bottom step and the full-frontal, full impact hit with a *wow*. It was as if a flashbulb went off and Olivia blinked. There he was. A fully formed, three-dimensional, reach-out-with-both-hands-and-touch example of prime masculinity.

The stranger she'd *not* promised Brie she'd stay away from.

A mouth-watering stranger with bronzed olive skin that tempted any woman with a pulse to lick her way across that shadowed chin and linger awhile at the perfectly sculpted mouth.

His gaze met hers as if she'd summoned him to look her way. And he didn't look pleased about that. His eyebrows lowered, his mouth firmed and a muscle clenched in his jaw.

He looked kind of familiar but she'd totally have remembered a guy like him. She'd revelled in that initial instant of feminine power but now somehow he'd reversed the situation and that cool control she could always count on, and was so proud of, was disappearing like ice on a barbecue grill.

Steely black eyes with the power to tempt. To persuade. A shiver rippled down her spine. The power to take her will and flex it between his long slender fingers like so much overcooked spaghetti.

And Olivia felt hot, as she did when standing on the steaming deck of her yacht on a midsummer's day in Barbados. In the eye of a tropical storm even, because her usually strong sea legs were wobbly.

She was still looking at him and he was still looking at her and she swore she saw him mouth, 'Trouble'.

Oh yeah, absolutely. Double trouble in flashing neon lights. She'd never met a man who'd affected her this way—this hot, itchy, melty way. Not that they'd met... Had they?

Her pulse took off and her heart raced to catch up. He'd moved so subtly she hadn't noticed that he stood between her and the only route to the lower levels via the marble staircase. Intentional or not—she couldn't be sure and the anticipation hummed through her body like a build-up of static electricity.

Fight or flight? In yachting there was only one option. Unexpected and dangerous situations were dealt with in a calm, rational manner. Dealing with men was no different. Whatever happened, she would *not* run away.

With feigned indifference, she tossed her bedraggled twist of feathers over one shoulder, a silky strand catching on her lip as she drew in a wheezy breath to say, 'Hi.'

Jett knew it was time to leave when Trouble with the most eye-catching, reddest hair he'd ever seen spoke to him in that husky, breathless voice. But he couldn't tear his eyes away from the feather stuck to her pouty lower lip as she made little *puh-puh* noises to try and blow it off. He had the weirdest image of her blowing those little noises on his belly while her fingernails raked over his nipples and her hands swirled over his chest, his hips. Lower.

Damn.

Just say hi back and walk away. Fast. But his feet obeyed only that rapidly hardening part of his anatomy, and before he knew it he'd crossed the space between them, reached out and plucked the feather from what was a very pretty mouth. He felt a sensation of warm static before he snatched his fingers back.

'Thanks.' Eyes the colour of his signature Blue Mint Lagoon cocktail sparkled.

He curled tingling fingers into a fist. Another damn. Trouble with a sense of humour.

He saw…something…behind the fun and she looked away quickly, as if she hadn't meant to share. Her gaze flicked upwards and behind him. 'Anything interesting up there?'

There could be—if you want. 'Nope.'

'There has to be *something*, or why the staircase?'

He shrugged at her logic, stuck his hands in his trouser pockets. 'Just a couple of telescopes.'

'Really? I love stargazing.'

Even in the dimness he could see the fairy lines fanning out from the corners of her eyes and a splash of freckles over her nose. She enjoyed the outdoors whereas he rarely had the time for such indulgence. No doubt another spoiled socialite with plenty of time to waste. 'Too much light pollution in the city,' he told her, rocking back on his heels. 'I'd say they're for watching the harbour.'

'Oh, yes, why didn't I think of that?'

She walked to the bottom of the spiral stairs and peered up, one slender hand on the rail. Sun-kissed skin. Neat unvarnished nails. A nice flash of abundant cleavage. Man, he had to stop staring like some pre-pubescent teenager—

'Did you sneak a peek?'

'What?' His guilty gaze shot somewhere over her shoulder, then he realised she was talking about *telescopes*. 'Ah... no.'

She cast him an unreadable look then started up. 'Why not?'

'Because— Hey, you won't want to go up like that.' In one stride he was there, his fingers closing firmly over hers. The contact sent a zing up his forearm. All that static build-up discharged in one hit.

She must have felt it too because her eyes widened and her mouth dropped open. 'Like...what?'

He yanked his hand away. 'Those heels—you'll break your neck.'

'Only if I—' On cue, one stiletto slipped and caught in the iron lace doyley tread. She yanked it free. 'Cripes. I see your point.'

He shook his head. 'Why don't you—?'

'Okay...' On the third tread, she toed off her shoes. And

groaned lustily—a sound that did dangerous things to his already wide-awake libido. 'Relief at last. Why didn't I think of that earlier?' She handed them to him over the rail, avoiding skin contact. 'Hold these till I get back.'

'I…' Siren-red patent, they were warm from her feet and smelled of new leather. Dangling them from one hand, he watched her climb, toenails painted to match, strong toned calves. Smooth, golden thighs disappeared beneath the shadows of her dress's short hemline. She moved fast and without effort, as if she worked out a lot. A yachtie's woman?

If Jett were the skipper, he'd keep her below decks and all to himself for the entire journey. Yep, naked and barefoot—he could get creative with feet, a little warm brandy and sweet ripe apricots—

Hell. He shook his head to clear it. Now was *not* the time to be coming up with new recipes.

He wasn't looking for a woman, dammit. He had to remind himself again because his mind seemed to have forgotten. He was waiting for Breanna, half-sister, who was doing whatever, with whomever. Everything, it seemed, except checking in with him. He should go back to the hotel, catch up on some sleep. Away from trouble in a red dress.

But he had her shoes. He could hardly just abandon them here. And he didn't want to leave without one more glimpse of her. Which wasn't quite true because he wanted more than a glimpse. A lot more.

He placed one foot on the bottom step and made an instant decision. Forget Breanna; she hadn't answered his call. Instead, a little up-close and personal might just be on the menu for tonight. No trouble, he assured himself; he didn't want or need to know who she was. A hot lick of anticipation stroked down his body and his steps quickened while his stomach tightened and his mouth watered. One sweet taste. The perfect dessert to end the evening.

* * *

Olivia hoped the sound of her heart pounding its way out of her chest wasn't audible. Hearing his footsteps on the metal treads, she turned as the guy appeared on the platform behind her. And was blown away again by the sight of all that blatant masculinity. Which was unsettling because she'd relegated men to the bottom of her list of priorities a long time ago.

Determined not to let him see how much he was affecting her, she moved to the larger telescope and adjusted it for a view of the party-goers milling around Circular Quay to distract herself and give her time to think what to do next.

She could feel his gaze stroking heat down her spine and the backs of her thighs. His musky masculine scent wafted her way. As diversions went, the impromptu viewing idea was an epic fail—she had no idea if the lens was in focus or not. As for coming up with what to do next, heck, all she could think was how his lips would taste... 'Amazing,' she murmured.

'Have to agree with you there.'

She turned to him but he wasn't looking at the twinkling carpet of lights on the harbour, he was watching her and screwing with her equilibrium again. She deflected with, 'Are you sailing in the race?'

'Not me.'

She noticed he didn't ask the same of her. No doubt the women he associated with were willowy, fragile types who were afraid of breaking a fingernail or a sweat. 'Sailing's not your thing?'

He shrugged, his hands in his trouser pockets. 'In case you're wondering, I'm here for the free food.'

She laughed spontaneously. 'Ah, it was you who demolished all the prawns.' She gestured to the crowd on the dance floor below who were swaying their hips and waving their little gold bells to 'Jingle Bell Rock'. 'So, were you getting your groove on down there on the dance floor tonight?'

He shook his head, a smile on his lips. 'I'm not the prawn thief and since you didn't ask me to dance, no, I wasn't.' And oh, my, in the shadowy light, the cutest, *innocent-little-boy* dimples flirted at the corners of his mouth. It kick-started some sort of weird maternal instinct when what it should have been doing was to warn her to run in the opposite direction.

Between talking up Snowflake to anyone who'd listen, she'd danced her feet to death—*and* had continued to promote Snowflake while bopping. 'I didn't see you…' Men never joked with her, but this one was—at least she *thought* he was—and she trailed off, feeling awkward.

'Haven't been here long,' he told her at last. 'Anyway the Macarena's not really my thing.'

'Not even the Christmas Macarena with the jingle bells and reindeer antlers to wiggle along with?'

'I don't do Christmas.' He walked to the railing, gazed at the harbour.

'No?' she said to his back. 'What, like, you don't do the whole mistletoe, eggnog, Secret Santa thing—or is it a personal belief?'

'Two words: Christmas commercialism.' When he turned to her, his eyes had lost their spark.

She wasn't buying it—something had happened in his past that had nothing to do with Christmas commercialism.

'It doesn't have to be,' she said. 'Unless you let it.'

He shrugged. 'Anyway, who needs mistletoe? If you want to kiss someone you should go ahead and kiss them, wouldn't you agree?' He seemed to lean towards her. 'Why wait for Christmas?'

Why, indeed? He *had* leaned towards her. 'It depends on whether that person wants to be kissed.' She told herself she didn't. She *wished* she didn't but, oh, she really did. Every muscle in her body tightened and softened and her lips were practically puckering up in anticipation. 'But a little festive smooch beneath the mistletoe's always fun.' *And infinitely safer than shadowed, secluded corners.*

Dark brows rose. 'Always?' Somehow, as if she'd willed it, he was within touching distance. She could feel the heat radiating from his body, like runaway power from a nuclear reactor. His eyes seared her with dark intensity.

'Usually,' she amended with a laugh that sounded nervous to her own ears. 'With a few Christmas drinks under one's belt and everyone bursting with good cheer, it's harmless enough.' Unlike that nuclear reaction approaching critical mass in the narrowing space between them.

Had she said *harmless*? It was a foregone conclusion; this virtual stranger was going to kiss her and she was going to let him and excitement tingled through her body like a swarm of hungry fire ants.

'So convince me Christmas is worth all the fuss,' he murmured, reaching out and fingering the ends of her hair.

She wondered that she couldn't smell the singe in the air and had to fight for her composure again. 'Where do you want me to begin?'

'Refresh my memory and run that Secret Santa bit by me again. Is it the same as Kris Kringle?'

'Not necessarily,' she decided, and ventured into uncharted waters. 'First off...' she reached up on tiptoe, slid her boa around his neck then stepped backwards, letting it slide through her fingers until she was holding the very ends '...and most importantly...' she met his eyes boldly even though her legs felt as though they were stumbling through sand '...it has to be a secret.'

'Trust me, I won't tell a soul.' His voice was silk seduction, sliding over her and all but stealing away any sense she might have had.

'Trust you? Where are my shoes, by the way?'

'Safe.' He glanced down between their bodies then back to her face. 'I like you barefoot.'

'So do I, it's so liberating, don't you think?' Something danced behind his smouldering gaze and her feet tickled—as if he were sucking them right into his mouth. One toe at a time. 'You'd be my Secret Santa?'

'For you...' he ran one lazy fingertip over her left collarbone, making her shiver '...I could be persuaded. Are you sleeping with anyone?'

The question came out of nowhere and he spoke casually, as if he were asking whether she liked sugar in her coffee. A tugging sensation she'd never experienced unfurled low in her belly and her cheeks burned with fire. 'Not that it's any of your business.' Confusion warred with irritation at his smooth, almost lazy arrogance.

'It is if I'm going to kiss you the way I want to kiss you.' His fingertip moved from her collarbone to skim across her lower lip.

Her lips burned and the low tugging sensation pulled into a tight knot. Her habitual defensiveness evaporated. What was it about this man that she'd throw away any sense of caution?

She'd obviously been struck by some random insanity.

Over the years, she'd grown accustomed to guys accusing her of being intimidating or closed off. Snowflake and her studies had taken her focus and consumed her energy for so long it hadn't left time for anything else, particularly any fleeting and indulgent liaisons with the opposite sex. She had more important things on her agenda, such as making a difference for people with serious and terminal illness.

But it was Christmas Eve and random insanity had indeed

struck because right now on the top of this year's Christmas list was his lips on hers. Her Secret Santa—dark as midnight, and an exciting mystery to unravel and enjoy. Just for tonight.

He watched her, reading her thoughts. Knowing she was going to say yes. But then he said, 'When a woman tells me it's none of my business, it's usually because she wants me to kiss her regardless of the man she's sleeping with.'

Oh, he was cocky, arrogant, full of himself. An irate breath caught in her throat. 'Of course I'm not sleeping with anyone or I wouldn't be standing here with you.' She drew herself up tall. 'And if you think I'm that kind of woman then you have very poor taste and we have nothing in common.'

'On the contrary, I have very discerning taste when it comes to women. If I thought you were lying you wouldn't see me for dust.'

She relaxed a bit, if you could call letting out a slow breath and sucking in another relaxing. 'Good, then. Because...because I want you to kiss me...that way.'

His mouth quirked and he touched the ends of her hair again as the band struck up their version of 'All I Want for Christmas'. 'Glad we cleared that up.'

'Me too.'

'Now, where were we?'

She licked dry lips. 'Secret Santa.'

'Ah...' The devil with a smile lurked in his black eyes as his hands slid up her bare arms to her shoulders.

The hairs on her arms rose in response and she shivered and met his gaze. 'Except you look like more of a sinner than a Santa.'

He pulled the top half of her body into stunning and breath-stealing contact, his lips tantalisingly close to hers. 'Which do you want me to be?'

CHAPTER TWO

OF COURSE THE GUY was a mind-reader as well because he knew her instant preference for sin over safe and his body hardened against hers and his fingers tightened on her arms. Up close Olivia could see gold stardust in his irises and her own desire reflected back.

And heaven help her, wild and wicked was exactly what she needed tonight. She wanted to lose herself to oblivion. To dive headlong into those dark depths and surrender to the promised pleasure she saw there—

Except...this whole scenario was straight out of her private fantasies but now it was real and happening and moving too fast and she couldn't catch her breath.

'Wait.' She dragged a hand up between them, pushed it against his chest. Hard as concrete. But warm and sculpted, and to her dismay her fingers spread over the undulating surface of their own volition. 'Just. Wait.'

'Are you okay?' He loosened his hold and leaned back. 'Because if you're not s—'

'I'm fine.' She sucked in air. 'Absolutely fine.' Or would be if she could establish the same footing with this godlike, devilishly attractive being in front of her. *Not* surrender, she told herself. Equality.

'Tell you what,' he said, slowly. 'Why don't we—?'

'Yes. Why don't we?' And before she changed her mind

again she wound her fingers around the ends of her boa for a firm hold. Here was a rare chance to grab life and living with both hands and reel him in. She saw the glimpse of surprise in his dark eyes as she reached up on tiptoe, yanked him close and planted her mouth on his.

And oh, this man didn't disappoint. As their lips connected she was sure she heard a hiss. More of a sizzle, actually. Heat met heat and that smouldering spark that had been arcing between them since they'd first laid eyes on each other ignited. She felt it catch, deep down inside, sending showers of sparkles to every extremity.

He pulled back a fraction. 'Is control your thing, darling?' A rogue's smile danced over his lips and his eyes lit with amusement.

In a different situation his condescending *darling* would have annoyed her, but she didn't have time to be annoyed because he was already moving his lips over hers once more and playing the game—his way. He was mayhem and magic and completely irresistible.

Determined to keep up, she matched his enthusiasm, leaning in and arching her body against his. Their lips softened and parted. Merged. His flavour invaded her mouth as breath mingled, tongues met and entwined.

She tasted wealth and power and persuasion. Danger in a will that matched her own. And for the first time in her life she wondered if a man—specifically, *this* man—might be more than she could handle.

But this was just a little harmless flirtation on a balcony. And Christmas Eve was about midnight madness and whimsical delights.

With eager hands she acquainted herself with his body. Hard slabs of muscle, the soft indent below his Adam's apple. The springy masculine hair that sprouted from the V of his open-necked shirt. He was a gift and she was a kid on Christmas morning.

His hands were busy too, warm and firm on her shoulders, beneath her hair, down her back, toying with the top of her zipper. She gave an involuntary shiver—the tiny metal teeth were the only things holding up her dress and preventing her from standing here in nothing but red lace bikini panties.

On a balcony metres away from a hundred or more guests.

With a man she didn't know.

Someone had so spiked that cocktail.

Or maybe it was time to live on the edge for once.

Damn. Jett managed, with difficulty, to pry his lips from hers. 'I knew it.' He leaned back and searched her face through a fog of lust. 'Was that a *fun* shiver of delight and anticipation or do we need the festive foliage?'

'Definitely fun.' She smiled, those effervescent starlight eyes sparkling. 'No mistletoe required.'

'Thank God for that, then; I've no idea where to find any.'

'What did you mean by: *you knew it*?' she asked.

He hadn't intended to say it aloud and blamed it on working all day after last night's all-hours drink-fest. He slid his hands over lush feminine curves, lingering on her hips. 'That you'd be a refreshing surprise at the end of a very ordinary day.'

Her hands covered his. 'Not trouble?'

He touched his nose to hers. 'You're big trouble.'

'I can live with that.' Unrepentant, she entwined their fingers and rubbed her lips over his. 'How about you?'

He sucked her sweet taste from his lips. 'Mmm…' Strawberries and pineapple with a dash of vodka. 'So can I,' he murmured before leaning down for a second helping.

More of this out-of-control feeling he'd not experienced

since his teens. His erection throbbed and ached and burned as if it were his first time. His head spun with the fragrance of her skin, her hair and the way she shifted against him—breasts, belly, thighs all aligned perfectly, as if she'd been made to order. It wasn't his lack of sleep sending him slightly insane—it was her.

Crazy was good—so were her lips: warm and pliant and mobile. He'd been working manic hours for months now; he needed a change of pace and didn't everyone need a bit of wholesome crazy now and then? As she said, it was Christmas. It wasn't called the silly season for nothing. 'Maybe there's something in this Secret Santa business after all,' he murmured into her ear.

Her cheek lifted into a smile against his. 'Definitely,' she agreed, winding slender arms that smelled of sun-warmed apricots and cool cucumber around his neck.

With a growl, he walked her backwards until she butted up against the wall. He might have stopped a moment to admire the Titian-haired picture of perfection before him but patience had never been one of his strengths when it came to beautiful, willing women. He ground his pelvis against her and was rewarded when she arched her hips in response and sent up a little whimper of longing and capitulation. Her fingernails dug into his shoulders and she moaned.

'Yes, darling, I've got what you want.' One hand cupped the back of her head to hold her in place while he continued to savour the sweet delight of her mouth, the other glided over a breast, finding a taut little bead that hardened instantly beneath his touch.

He rolled it between his fingers through the fabric and she moaned again—the soft yielding sound compelling him to put his lips there. His teeth. To nip at the silk, to close his mouth over the bud and suck. To soothe her while he tortured himself with what he couldn't do. At least, not here.

But the sounds of the party below seemed muted and irrelevant in the shadows. He looked into her desire-drenched eyes while he smoothed his palms over her dress, sliding the skin-warmed silk up her thighs. Up, over her hips. 'You like what I'm doing to you.'

She pressed her lips together but a little mewing sound escaped.

'There's more,' he promised, his fingers finding and exploring the smooth flesh of her inner thighs. Her head rolled back against the wall and her eyes darted towards the stairs. 'No one's going to come up here,' he reassured her in his best persuasive tone. 'Trust me.'

Wide-eyed, she looked back at him, disbelief etched between her slim brows. Her arms slid down to her sides, apparently incapable of holding on any longer.

Satisfaction rolled through him. She was his. Or would be, before the night was done.

'Hey,' he murmured, inching his hand higher, drawing tiny circles with his fingertips and feeling her legs start to tremble. 'You chose sinner over Santa, work with me here.'

She shook her head. 'I…'

'A good choice.' His fingers found satin and lace. *Hot and damp* satin and lace, and he knew they were halfway to where they both wanted to go.

But then she tensed. Sucked on her bottom lip.

'Hey, it's Christmas,' he teased gently.

'But—'

He cut off her protest with a slow, soothing kiss until he felt her soften once more. 'Okay, forget sinner,' he said against her lips. 'We'll play Secret Santa instead, and he won't do anything you don't want him to. You're in the driver's seat, and a few dozen guests within earshot over the balcony will tell you the same.'

In the driver's seat? Olivia might have laughed but she

was half out of her mind. Delirious and blinded by a desire and an urgency she'd never experienced.

A mistake, that cocktail, because she should have been able to resist. She'd never had a problem resisting men. But this man wasn't just any man. He was wicked and persuasive and clever, and his hand was *inside* her panties, touching her—thrilling her—with just one flick of his finger over her most sensitive place and any second now she was going to shatter into a million pieces and she knew she'd never be the same ever again.

'Come for me.' The voice at her ear transported her to undiscovered realms, lifting her higher to some pinnacle just beyond her reach—

The distinctive beat of Coldplay jolted her back to some vague resemblance of reality. *Brie.* With trembling fingers she yanked her phone from the jewelled bag slung over one shoulder. Brie's picture smiled at her. She glared back, found her voice. '*Now* you call.'

His fingers stilled but his hand remained, hot and arousing and slippery, inside her panties. 'Is it an emergency?'

'I don't think so, b—'

'Then get rid of whoever it is.'

His dictatorial tone irritated. 'No.' However tempting, she couldn't—*wouldn't*—ignore her friend until she knew she was okay. 'I have to get this.'

Reluctantly, she tried to push his hand away. It didn't budge. In the end she had no choice but to answer—breathlessly. 'Hi…' She closed her eyes as if not seeing him would somehow make him disappear. Resisted squirming against his fingers—for all of three seconds or so. 'You all right?'

'I'm great. Fabulous. What took you so long to answer?'

Brie wasn't the only one feeling fabulous. 'I'm…' what the hell, Brie would be happy for her '…being seduced by a man in black. He's my Secret Sinner-Santa.'

'Believe it,' he whispered into her ear.

She pressed her lips together to stop the urge to smile and squeal at the same time and felt the scrape of his bristled jaw against her neck.

Pause at the other end of the phone. 'Oh. Okay. Sorry I'm late but I'm here now. Are you still at the party? I've looked everywhere.'

Not quite everywhere, Brie. 'Yes…' *Omigod*… His thumb was doing something amazing. How could she think, let alone carry on any semblance of intelligent conversation while he manipulated her with such devastating expertise? Darts of pleasure were shooting through her body and lights were coalescing and swirling in front of her eyes. 'Still… here. Already told you…'

'Where?' Irritated impatience.

'I'm…not…good company right now.'

'I disagree,' murmured the muffled voice, this time against the top of her breasts.

'What?' Brie's voice, confused. 'Is there someone with you?'

'Must be…the hand—*the band*.' A breeze with scent of summer and sex cooled the raging inferno in her cheeks while Secret Sinner-Santa assumed control and drove her to a rising crescendo of delight and desire and sheer desperation with every manic beat of her pulse.

'And what do you mean *not good company*? Ken's waiting, stay right where you are, wherever it is, I'm coming to get you.'

'No… *I'm* coming…'

And she was. Right now. Right here. Awareness narrowed down to a pinpoint of sparkling sensation and the hand holding her phone slid from her ear as the world receded like the tide before a tsunami.

She heard the disembodied moan—part plea, all pleasure—sprint up her throat as the crescendo peaked and rolled, sending her tumbling over the silvery crest and showering her body with gold.

A slow sigh escaped her lips. Sweet, sugar-coated bliss. Sagging against his hard-packed stomach and an impressive erection, she floated down, her feet still not quite touching the ground. She wasn't exactly a virgin but no guy had ever done it for her the way he had. Now she understood how sinfully, devastatingly irresistible the right man's touch could be.

On the downside, it reduced even the most rational, self-disciplined person to a quivering, mindless mass. It had changed a sane sensible woman with a mind and opinion of her own—and an ability to say no—to someone she didn't recognise.

She flopped her head back against the wall and looked up at him, committing his face to memory, then kissed her fingers and pressed them to his lips. 'Merry Christmas.'

From somewhere near her left elbow, she heard Brie's voice. 'Olivia, are you *drunk*?'

'No.' Just not herself. Without taking her eyes off him—the way a sailor wouldn't take her eyes off an approaching storm front—she raised the phone to her ear. 'Meet you on the driveway. Two minutes.'

She disconnected and began sidestepping along the wall. Away. Now she'd had a moment to come to her senses, all she wanted was to be by herself and think about what she'd done. What *he'd* done. *Oh my God*. Her inner muscles clenched in fond remembrance. Casual sex on a balcony was *not* who she was. She didn't know what to say, so she went with, 'Thanks.'

He caught her arm, his dark, almost familiar eyes a cool shade of cynical. 'So that's it? *Thanks?*'

'Yes. What else do you want me to say?'

His nostrils flared and a muscle twitched along his jaw. 'We haven't finished.'

Oh. She couldn't help it; her gaze flicked down between them and her whole body felt weak and fizzy at the tempting display of manly magnificence outlined in fine black fabric. Pity she wasn't going to see it in all its glory. 'Sorry. I am, truly.' *You'll never know how much.* 'But my friend's waiting.'

He remained where he was, expression dangerously impassive. 'Better hurry, then. And watch your step.'

A shiver ran down her spine but she realised he hadn't meant it as a threat but a warning to take care on the stairs. Hiding his annoyance that she was running off without so much as a name uttered between them. Or was he relieved, as she was, that this had just been a little harmless Christmas Eve flirtation? No, she very much doubted he felt relieved.

Coldplay started up again, making her jump. 'Thirty seconds, Brie, and I'm there,' she said to the phone. 'Have you met up with Jett yet?' She was proud of her casual question and breezy voice as she all but stumbled to the stairs, scrambling for the handrail and tripping over her feet on her way down, a pair of eyes following her every move. She could feel them, dark and intense down her spine.

'Forget Jett,' Brie told her in a tight-lipped voice. 'He's obviously forgotten *me*. He can damn well find his own way back.'

Olivia slowed her mad dash when she saw Brie pacing the circular drive beside their chauffeured car. But not soon enough, because Brie had caught sight of her first. One slim eyebrow hiked and a smile played around her lips. Taking in Olivia's no-doubt ravished and guilty-as-sin appearance.

'Let's go,' Olivia said, pulling her evening bag off her shoulder and crushing it between her fingers.

Brie didn't move. '*Sinner-Santa*, Liv. You weren't kidding after all.'

'It's Christmas.' The car was idling, the door was open and Olivia moved fast. 'What are we waiting for?'

'Such a hurry.' Brie stepped into her path, sharp eyes scanning Olivia's bare feet. 'Cinderella only lost one shoe.'

Oh. *Crap.* 'Never mind.' She darted around Brie, muttering, 'Thanks, Ken,' and sweeping past their driver as if the hounds of hell were about to catch up with her. 'What's a pair of shoes?'

She piled into the back seat, her pesky observant friend settled in beside her, and Ken closed the door. Brie pressed a button and the privacy screen rose. As the vehicle progressed sedately towards the gates she picked a feather off Olivia's shoulder, held it up as evidence. 'And where's the rest of my boa?'

Leaning back against the head rest, Olivia closed her eyes, which only drew attention to the riot happening inside her. 'There was a wink in those words, Brie. And a nudge. And I'm warning you now they won't get you anywhere.'

She felt the seat dip as Brie shifted towards her. 'BFFs share.'

'There's nothing to share.' Blood rushed to Olivia's cheeks. 'Not a thing.'

'Well, fa-la-la-la-la!' She punctuated each meaningfully loaded syllable with an exclamation mark. 'Not a thing, hmm?'

She blew out a resigned breath. 'Okay, not quite not a thing.'

'Not quite?'

'No. Yes. No. Doesn't matter.'

'What's his name and are you seeing him again?'

'No to both.'

'Oh.' Brie sounded disappointed. Olivia's emotions were

so all over the place she didn't know how she herself felt. 'And if I did know his name, I wouldn't tell you. Big fat *huh* to BFFs. You haven't talked to me about Jett, so we're even.'

'Jett's my brother, not my lover, it's hardly the same. And if you must know, I haven't talked about Jett because he asked me not to.'

'Why? Oh, Brie, he's not done something, like, really bad, has he?' She remembered Brie talking about his reluctance to open up and dropped her voice to a whisper. 'Like, has he been in prison...?'

'No.' Brie laughed. 'Nothing like that. But he's in the media—'

'Famous?' Olivia nodded slowly. 'I'd know him.'

'Livvie, you've been so focused on your work and studies and getting Snowflake up and going these past few years, I doubt it. And you really know how to deflect the conversation away from you.'

'I told you. Okay, I didn't tell you.' She lowered the window to let the breeze cool her face. 'We didn't... But he... I...' She smiled—she couldn't help it. 'It truly was an orgasmic experience.'

'Wow.'

'Totally.' But Olivia's buoyancy faded and something not so cheerful hooked in her chest. She pushed it away hard and joked, 'Sinner-Santas are strictly for Christmas Eve. They disappear in a twinkle of Santa's sleigh bell at midnight. And...' she checked her watch '...Christmas Eve's over.'

It was officially Christmas Day. The two of them were supposed to be having Christmas lunch with the mysterious brother—if he bothered to turn up. And Boxing Day it was all hands on deck, meaning if he didn't show Brie wouldn't catch up with him for days. 'You've heard nothing from Jett?'

She gave a tight shrug. 'He texted he was on his way to the party. Since then, nothing.'

'He knows you're in the race, doesn't he?'

'Yeah. He was coming to Sydney anyway, so I suggested we could celebrate the festive day together. Maybe it wasn't a good idea.'

'He'll turn up, Brie. And I can't wait to meet him.'

Well, if that didn't take the celebration cake. Jett watched her flee, red hair flying, relieved he hadn't gone any further. Still, it could've been an even hotter night in the city—if he hadn't found out who she was. He shifted his stance to accommodate the swelling in his trousers that wasn't likely to subside any time soon.

Trouble in strawberry lace D-cups. In the flesh.

And there'd been an abundance of that. Smooth and creamy and *damn*. Dragging off the feathers she'd left around his neck, he stuffed them in his back pocket. He could smell her skin—apricots and cucumber.

He might have followed, if only to return her shoes—then persuade her that the festivities should be extended a few hours because it was still Christmas Eve somewhere in the world—until he'd heard her mention his name. *His* name.

He'd been fooling around with Breanna's friend.

A harsh bark of laughter escaped. What were the odds? Walking to the balcony, he searched out the driveway mostly hidden by a corner of the house. He caught sight of Breanna in the car's headlights. He didn't have to wait long to see a flash of red zip past her and disappear into the car.

The car accelerated down the drive and he turned away, facing into the breeze blowing up from the harbour. He needed to cool off. One minute without an audience—he shifted again—better make that five minutes. The excruciating pity of it all was she'd had no idea who he was and he might have enjoyed an evening—and a hell of a lot more—with someone who wasn't out for his name and fame.

Breanna's friend.

Sexy.

Available.

Not a good idea.

He scowled at the wall where she'd come apart beneath his hand, dress hiked, thighs quivering and her moans of pleasure sobbing on the air. The scent of her arousal lingered. Hell. He'd be lucky if he slept a wink tonight.

He'd known she was trouble the instant he'd clapped eyes on her.

But—he couldn't help but grin—trouble had never come in such a tempting package.

CHAPTER THREE

'THIS IS THE LIFE.'

After five days of hard slog on the harbour, Olivia was enjoying a traditional Christmas Day breakfast of champagne, strawberries and Danish pastries while a little light Christmas music played in the background. She wasn't accustomed to inactivity but two days of R and R were well deserved and a necessary break before the hard work, both mental and physical, that the next few days would demand of them.

Brie, looking as boneless as Olivia felt on the other recliner, studied the forest-green lacquered toenails as she wiggled them in front of her. 'This is so not the life; you'd be bored to distraction in a couple of days.'

'True. I should wander down to the gym in a bit.'

'Nuh-uh.' Brie nibbled on a croissant. 'No workouts allowed today.'

Olivia flopped back, almost relieved. She'd barely slept after all. 'If you say so.'

Jeez, she was so easily seduced. *Seduced. Workout...* Hot, steamy, sweaty— 'The pool, then. A quick twenty laps.'

Brie lifted her sunglasses off her nose to stare at her. 'After this feast? I don't think so. You're just feeling the twitchy after-effects of last night's indulgence with Secret Sinner-Santa.'

A shiver of remembered delight danced down her spine and settled low and warm between her thighs. 'You are so right. I never knew sinning was that much fun.'

'Woo-hoo, now you do.'

She'd been involved short-term with a guy a long time ago and it had been more about a loss of innocence than sinning—or even enjoyment, because with Jason there hadn't been much enjoyment, for her at least. But since she and Brie had met at the hospice where Brie's dad and Olivia's mum were dying, she'd been so focused on getting Pink Snowflake up and running and her plans for a retreat, she'd had no time for guys, relationships. Sex.

But last night... Olivia smiled. He'd whetted her appetite. It was as if that dormant part inside her had finally woken up and demanded breakfast.

'He was good, then?'

She sighed. 'The man had *the best* hands. *And* he knew how to use them.' She smiled, lost for an instant, reliving the pleasure. Heat spurted through her lower belly and she reached for her glass of sparkling mineral water. 'The fact that he was built like a god was a bonus. He had these eyes...' She blinked the images—him—away. He was long gone.

And switched topics. 'So Jett made it back here eventually.' She'd heard him come in after she and Brie had said goodnight and had been tempted to go pour herself a glass of water from the kitchenette, just to sneak a peek. But she'd changed her mind when she heard their muffled voices through her closed door. She'd not wanted to intrude. 'Was he lost?'

'I don't think so.' Brie stirred her coffee. 'What I can't work out is that he said he'd made it to the party late and all would become clear.'

'That's cryptic,' Olivia said.

'Good morning.'

The deep male voice had Olivia pushing upright and turning to the open doorway. 'Hi...' As she spoke her smile dropped away; her entire body started to dissolve.

How had he known where to find her? *What are you doing here?* But the words never passed her frozen lips because even as she asked the question she knew the answer.

Jett.

Her not-so-secret Sinner-Santa.

One and the same and ambling away from the door as if he'd been leaning casually against it. Listening in. Laughing at her. Looking so, so smug. Every indignant hair on the back of her neck rose and she pushed suddenly sweaty hands over her trembling thighs and down the skirt of her festive emerald-trimmed white sundress.

He wore khaki shorts and a white polo shirt and brown sandals. Plenty of bare leg sprinkled with dark masculine hair. Then she caught sight of a pair of red stiletto sandals set neatly on the floor beside the door frame.

Brie didn't notice the incriminating evidence and rose. 'Jett, glad to see you're awake at last. Did you sleep well?'

'Not bad.' His eyes flicked to Olivia. 'Considering.'

The eyes. Brie's eyes, Olivia realised, seeing the pair of them close together. How had she missed that? Both tall and equally stunning with their bronzed complexions and midnight gazes. Brie leaned in and pecked him on the cheek. 'Merry Christmas.' She turned to Olivia. 'Jett, I want you to meet my best friend, Olivia Wishart. Liv, this is Jett Davies. My brother.'

He nodded to Olivia and a corner of his mouth quirked. 'Already had the pleasure.'

At the mention of pleasure, fingers of guilty heat stroked her belly and lower. How outrageous and inappropriate of him to mention it. Aware of the height disadvantage, she forced herself to stand. *Almost* eye to eye. Give or take a good six inches. But her legs felt like wet seaweed and the sun shimmered on all that bronzed masculine skin. Sliding on her sunglasses, she snapped out, 'It's always helpful to put a name to the face.'

'You two know each other?' Brie's gaze darted between the two of them then settled on Olivia, puzzled.

'Last night.' Jett fired the two words across the patio like an accusation or a challenge, then reached down beside him and swung the shoes on two fingers. 'You left these behind. Cinderella.'

She watched, appalled. Those same fingers had wrought wicked and unimaginable pleasure on her most intimate and private parts. When Olivia made no attempt to step forward and take them, he set them back by the door with a lazy grin, his eyes stroking down her body as if reacquainting himself with her shape, stopping at her bare feet. 'I'm sorry, were these your only shoes?'

'No.' She drew in a breath, embarrassed beyond belief, furious at his attitude. If Brie hadn't been there Olivia would have told him exactly where to put those shoes. 'Of course they're not. It's easy to forget—I'm a barefoot tragic.'

His lips pulled wide at that as if enjoying some private joke. 'I'll keep that in mind.'

'Whatever for?' She clenched her hands behind her back so he wouldn't see how they shook. Those little-boy dimples mocked her. And annoyed her—she doubted he'd ever been innocent in his life. 'Why are you *smirking*?'

Still grinning, he shrugged, lifting his arms to waist height, palms up. 'Why are you so uptight?'

'Olivia?' Brie's voice broke into their conversation. 'Can you help me in the kitchen a moment?'

'We don't have a kitchen here,' she reminded her, not taking her eyes off Jett. 'We have a private butler.' *And a problem.* She snatched up the magazine she'd been intending to read. 'Why don't you two catch up? I'm going to take that dip in the pool, then I'm going to shower and get ready for our yummy traditional Christmas feast. I expect you're looking forward to sharing Christmas lunch with Brie, Jett, as much as she's looking forward to sharing it with you.'

The force of her killer glare and unsubtle reference to Christmas luncheon rocked Jett back on his heels. 'You bet.' Still grinning, he watched her pick up her shoes, enjoying the rear view of touchable bottom and lightly honeyed thighs as she bent over. She stepped past the glass doors, into the entertainment area, skirted a low table where she dropped her magazine beside her boa, which he'd left there, then crossed the room and disappeared from view.

Man, she was hot. 'I guess she's mad at me. Must be the Christmas thing.'

'Christmas thing?' Brie murmured, following his gaze. 'Oh, you mean Secret Sinner-Santa—she mentioned it.'

That too.

'You didn't introduce yourselves?'

'Why would we? It was just a…' He trailed off. Probably not the wisest thing to say to the best friend. 'Should I try to—?'

'No. Sinner-Santas are for Christmas Eve—so I heard. I think if I was her, I'd want a little alone time. How long were you standing there?'

'Long enough.'

'Okay, here's the thing, Jett.'

She got real serious. It was always an unnerving experience with Breanna to be looking at his own eyes, and right now his sister's were clear and cool.

'Olivia's my best friend. She's also the most generous, caring person I know. She's been too busy studying and setting up her own charity and a dozen other activities over the past few years to have any sort of social life—and goodness knows she needs it. I can't remember the last time she—'

'What we get up to is between me and Olivia.'

'And that's fine with me. You're my brother, Jett, and I care about you. Whether or not you believe it, whether or not you want it, it's there and it's unconditional. But I care about Livvie too. She's like a sister to me. So be careful, okay?'

He felt awkward around sentimental words when they were directed his way and shrugged them off. 'Hey, it's cool. I don't need your care and concern, but thanks anyway.'

Her expression switched instantly and regret brimmed in eyes that looked at him as if he were a sick puppy. 'I can't forgive Dad for what he did.'

Ah. No. No way in hell was he getting into deep and meaningfuls with Breanna about their shared parentage. 'Forget it,' he muttered. He strode to a table sheltered by an umbrella. Ice clinked as he picked up a jug of chilled water.

'So as part of our familial connection,' she continued, while he poured himself a tall glass, and another for Breanna, 'I keep up with the press goings-on and your social-media updates. I know your fast and loose reputation with sophisticated women who know what the game's all about. A girl in every port.'

He held out one glass to Breanna and threw the contents of the other down his suddenly dry throat. *She'd kept tabs on him for the past three years?* Hell. 'So?' he said, meeting her gaze.

'Olivia's not like that.'

'You saying last night she wasn't herself, then?'

She waved her hands about her, unsure. 'I don't know about last night, I wasn't there. I'm just telling you what I know about who she is. How she is. Usually.'

'She's hardly talking to me as it is. Don't worry, I won't lay a finger on her. Or anything else.'

Unless she asks me to. He grew hard just thinking about last night and where his fingers had been. He refilled his glass and sat on one of the recliners to hide the incriminating evidence building a bonfire in his shorts. Yeah, any glimmer of reciprocation on the best friend's part and all bets were off.

Breanna took the other recliner. 'I'm not saying don't have a good time, Jett. She deserves some fun. She's in *desperate need* of some fun. But...' She shrugged, seemed to consider. 'Fine. You're both adults, I'll leave it up to you. And her.'

He nodded. 'It'll be okay,' he reassured her. 'You're racing tomorrow. I take it she's sailing with you?'

'Livvie's the reason I'm going. We've sailed together heaps.' She hugged her shoulders and smiled. 'I can't wait. It's turning out to be such a great Christmas.'

'Yeah.' His gaze flicked to the harbour, filled with myriad different craft on the white-flecked water, some decked with tinsel or coloured streamers. He'd never tell his sister he always spent the twenty-fifth of December doing anything so long as it wasn't related to Christmas.

When his trip to Thailand with a couple of mates had been cancelled at the last minute, he'd decided, on the spur of the moment, to accept Breanna's invitation to meet up in Sydney. He'd not realised he'd accepted the full Christmas Day deal until too late. She'd sounded so damn thrilled about it, he just hadn't been able to bring himself to disappoint her.

But she looked as if she was settling in for a bit of a sisterly chat so he said, 'Reckon I'll lie here and snooze for a bit.' He closed his eyes. 'Didn't get much sleep last night.'

She cleared her throat. 'Right. I'm going to take a shower.'

'Okay.' Which reminded him he'd been disappointed the

pretty strawberry underwear had disappeared when he'd used the second bathroom this morning.

The air was warm and muggy and he was dozing within moments...

...*Hurry up, Mummy.* She was always late to pick him up from school. Jett had got himself there this morning because he hadn't been able to wake her up. Again. He'd been so hungry he'd asked his teacher if he could have a Vegemite sandwich from the canteen, cos they did that sometimes when his mum didn't give him food cos she'd run out of money.

But then strangers came and took him away to another house and told him his mum had passed away. He wasn't sure what that meant but he knew he wouldn't be seeing her again and he cried heaps cos she'd told him she loved him and promised him that one day they'd go and live with his father in a big house and there'd be everything he'd ever wanted.

The lady that had picked him up told him he'd be living with other kids like him and he'd have lots of fun and make new friends. And he tried. But he didn't have fun and they picked on him cos he was smaller. So he fought back. And then they told him he was a trouble-maker and moved him to another place, then another. Who needed dumb friends anyway? He was waiting for the day his father came to get him, then everything would be okay.

And while he waited he dreamed how it was going to be. His father would laugh and open his arms and fold Jett in close like his mum used to do on her good days and tell him he'd been waiting for this day too.

Then one day they said his father wanted him to come for Christmas Day. He was overcome with breathless anticipation. Filled with wonder and excitement; his first proper Christmas with a real turkey and a tree and presents and stuff. His father might've got him a bike and he'd take him outside after lunch to teach him how to ride it and then he'd tell him he loved him and wanted him to stay for ever and that he had his own bedroom with a pirate bed and a pirate night light, cos he really liked pirates.

But when he got there, the man he'd dreamed about had sad eyes and didn't smile like how he'd imagined. He took him inside and there was a lady there too. Jett didn't understand why the lady wouldn't look at him or why she left the room with wet eyes. Then his father showed him a tiny bundle of baby with dark hair and eyes just like his own and told him her name was Breanna. His very own sister. And he forgot the man had looked sad cos now he was smiling and he let Jett touch the baby's skin and it felt like his mum's silk pillow case that she used to let him sleep on sometimes, only even softer. Today was the best day in the world.

But then the lady came and took the baby out of the room and his father told him that Jett couldn't be a part of his new family. Ever.

Jett stirred, rasped a hand over his stubble but kept his eyes closed. Christmas—and the old bad still followed like a dark shadow.

But his sister—the baby who'd ousted him from his rightful place in the family—was a bright light and not what he'd expected. He was still amazed that Breanna had come looking for him after their father had died and she'd learned she had an older brother. She'd been the sole heir to their father's estate but didn't seem to want anything from him but his friendship.

'You,' muttered a curt female voice. Just sharp enough to cut through the air and ensure he was listening, followed by the sound of fingertips drumming impatiently on the balcony rail.

His lips curved but his eyes remained closed. 'Hello, Trouble. Taking a few moment's down-time. Didn't get much sleep last night.'

'It's not your sleeping habits I'm bothered about.'

Her fresh apricot and cucumber scent wafted to his nostrils and he cracked open one eye. She'd showered; her gloriously red hair was damp and kissed elegant bare shoulders. A short black-and-white geometrically patterned dress hugged her curves. Curves he'd been getting intimately acquainted with not twelve hours ago. Curves he might have got even more intimate with if Breanna hadn't phoned Olivia and cut his plans for the rest of the evening short.

Breanna had phoned him too. Checked up on him. Left messages of concern, then annoyance. Which he probably should have answered but simply hadn't got around to.

Who the hell ever checked up on Jett Davies?

He caught Olivia glancing at him from beneath auburn lashes. She turned a pretty shade of watermelon pink when she saw him admiring her physical assets, then looked away and became preoccupied with counting the vehicles crossing the Harbour Bridge.

'You sure about that?' he said to her profile, his smile widening when he saw the increasing tension in her shoulders. 'My sleeping habits could be a good conversation starter. Why don't you sit down and we can discuss them?'

He'd half expected her to decline but she took a chair opposite him. 'As I was saying…it's your typical irresponsible male behaviour.'

'I am male,' he pointed out. 'I thought you'd have noticed last night. And yes, I'm pretty sure it was typical male behaviour when in the company of a sexy woman who wants the same thing he does. What I'm not sure about is the word irresponsible. I *have* heard of safe sex.'

She inhaled sharply, poured herself a glass of water from

the table beside her. 'You really have no idea what I'm talking about, do you?'

'But you're going to tell me.'

'Last night…'

'Last night…' He trailed off suggestively and the sultry images hung heavy in the air between them. He had an erection most men would be jealous of and nowhere to use it—damned if he was going to make it easy for her.

She cleared her throat, downed half the contents of her glass. 'It never occurred to you that Brie would be waiting to hear if you were okay, did it.' It wasn't a question. 'You never bothered to ring and let her know where you were.'

He flipped a hand. 'See, that's exactly why I don't keep women around long-term.' But he had to admit he saw her point.

'Brie's not just any woman, she's your sister. And I don't care what you do with your groupies, but you told Brie you were on your way to the party and that's the last she heard. While you were getting it on with some random woman she was worried about what might have happened to you.'

His brows rose. 'That woman was you.'

'*And* she felt let down because she'd been looking forward to sharing the evening with her brother. The fact it was me is irrelevant, Jett. Just because you're a famous chef-slash-food-writer-slash-critic—yes, Brie filled me in moments ago, and no, I didn't recognise you, which must be a blow to your over-inflated ego—doesn't mean you treat people who care about you that way. Accountability's obviously not a word you're familiar with and—'

'You sure have a lot to say.' Crikey, she was red hot when she was mad. Fiery. Filled with a vibrant energy to rival his own. It matched her hair and made him want to reach up, wind it around his fingers and pull her down so he could put that tongue to better use.

'When necessary, yes.'

'I get it.' He clicked his fingers. 'You're feeling bitchy because I got inside your panties and you loved every delicious second of it and now it's all over because you've decided that somehow it's not politically correct to mess around with your best friend's brother.'

Olivia blinked, her cheeks on fire. Because he had it so right. And she'd let her tongue run away from her. 'I'm not going to respond to that.'

'What, nothing to say now?' His voice held both humour and frustration. 'Or maybe it's because you know what I said is true.'

Her chin lifted. 'Plenty to say, but I'm resisting.'

'Like you did last night?' His expression was pained. 'Do you have any idea how *I* feel?'

Hot as molten steel and hard as concrete? She kept her gaze well away from his shorts. 'I said I was sorry.'

He nodded slowly, stared out at the harbour view. 'I'll apologise to Breanna.'

She nodded. 'Good.' She started to move to the balcony's glass doors. 'I think lunch is about ready. I'll go and check.' Escape.

'Wait up,' he said, and his hand shot out, curling around her elbow before she could blink. 'We'll check it out together.' Still holding her, he rose, all long loose limbs and lazy grace.

She went to step back, away, but his grip held her in place. His chest grazed her breasts and her nipples tightened into hard little bullets. It felt as if he were pinching them between his fingers the way he had last night and she bit back a moan.

This wasn't going her way at all. *Control, Olivia.* But his gaze was full of heated promises and she was already a devotee. She drew in a breath, her will dissolving like jelly. Racing heart, throbbing lips. Arousal like lava spurting through her veins and lower. A little sound rose up her throat and her face lifted itself to his. Just a kiss, she told herself. She could allow him—just once more. It was Christmas…

'Trouble,' he muttered, his lips so close to hers she could almost taste him. But not quite.

And then he smiled his wicked Sinner-Santa smile and walked inside, leaving her to follow. Or not.

No! She wanted to scream the word—and a few more explicit ones besides. To reach out and haul him back by his collar and give him a taste of real trouble. But she refused to let her personal problem with him interfere with a rare and happy family lunch.

The nerve of the man grated on her already tense nerves. Who was he to call *her* trouble? And in that sexual drawl that conjured up memories of when he'd called her that last night. Still, she only had to put up with him for a few hours. *So be nice a little longer. For Brie's sake.* Tomorrow they'd be oceans away.

CHAPTER FOUR

'DOES THE PRIME rib beef with Yorkshire pud meet your professional standards?' Brie asked Jett as the three of them worked their way through the scrumptious four-course silver-service luncheon served in their suite overlooking the famous harbour view.

Light reflected off water and danced across the ceiling and over crystal; a soft breeze fluttered the tinsel on the table decoration. The balmy air smelled of salt and roast dinner.

He topped up their champagne. 'I'm on vacation. The beef's tender, the pudding's puffed, browned and crisp, that's all I need to know.'

'Surely your professional taste buds never take a holiday?' Olivia suggested.

'No, but on occasion I like to eat without having to do an in-depth analysis. Like today.'

'Makes sense.' She nodded. 'Just indulge, enjoy and appreciate.'

Instant heat spurted up her neck. Wrong choice of words. *Wrong, wrong, wrong.* She focused on the stem of her glass while she twirled it on the tablecloth, but she knew his gaze was stroking over her and that he was interpreting those words in the context of their recent up-close and personal. 'I'm enjoying my grilled salmon,' she managed, desperately, then turned to her friend. 'How's the duck, Brie?'

Brie slipped a delicate mouthful past her lips. 'Perfection.'

Olivia mentally mimicked Brie's indulgent sigh. The duck wasn't the only perfection around here.

But was she the only one feeling the sudden lapse in conversation? Was it because they were too busy eating? Or maybe it was because the CD she'd put on earlier for just this possibility had come to an end...

Forcing herself to meet Jett's eyes, she said, 'So in your professional chef's opinion what's your most popular dish?'

He chewed a moment before answering. 'My soufflé is to die for. So I've been told.'

By a woman, she'd bet, judging by the way his mouth quirked and the little lines around his eyes crinkled when he answered. Possibly being fed from his spoon or while flat on her back. Or both. Not a scenario she wanted to think about. But she couldn't stop the tall, dark and delicious image flirting with her consciousness.

'You like soufflé?' Jett's question, spoken in that deep husky voice, those midnight eyes focused on her as if he'd read her mind...

'I tried to make it once. But it failed.' Cooking was her weakest skill and least favourite thing to do.

'You only gave it one shot?'

'Once was more than enough.'

'Persistence, Olivia,' he told her with a wink in his eye. 'Perfect timing's the key to good soufflé.' He regarded them both in turn while he chewed but Olivia sensed he was talking to her specifically when he said, 'You'll have to try my amaretto soufflé some time,' in a subtle way that stroked over her nape like the warm liqueur it was named for.

Brie's fork stopped halfway to her mouth. 'You're going to give us the famous Jettsetter Chef recipe? It's not in his books,' she told Olivia.

'How about I come and cook it for you some time? Show you how it's done?'

How about you do that? Olivia swallowed, the response turning her cheeks hot.

She should have recognised him from the photo inside the dust cover of *Sundae Night*. How could she not have picked up on the perfect bone structure and classic dark handsomeness? 'Brie gave me one of your books last Christmas.' She'd thought it was Brie's way to inspire Olivia's interest in cookery—now she knew better. Her best friend had kept him a secret… She raised her champagne flute. 'Now I know why it was a signed copy.'

'Did you enjoy it?' He added another dollop of horseradish sauce to his plate.

'It's got some delicious desserts.' And the added bonus of some sexy photos of the chef at work, but nowhere near clear enough to recognise him in the flesh. 'I do have to admit, though, that I've only tried out a couple.' She studied him a moment over the crystal rim. 'Do you ever get tired of cooking?'

'We've just finished filming a TV series to be shown later in the year, and, with the restaurant critiques, it's been full-on. I'm looking at some time-out so I'm working on ideas for themed cookbooks. Planning to start in Tasmania after the Taste Festival.'

At his mention of Hobart's premier summer event on the historic docks where the yacht race ended, Olivia said, 'If anyone can appreciate that particular festival, it's a chef.'

'I hope so.'

'Where to, then?'

'I've booked accommodation at Cradle Mountain.'

'Admit it, you must have had at least one cooking disaster in your lifetime.'

His lips twitched in amusement and his sinner's eyes teased. 'I don't recall.'

'Tell me about it anyway.' Olivia smiled back, and, awkwardness forgotten for the moment, she barely noticed Brie excuse herself and head out to the balcony with her glass of champagne.

Despite her earlier antagonism, she found herself drawn to him. The way he laughed with his eyes, his smooth way of talking, his hands. She couldn't seem to take her eyes off his hands, especially when he absently toyed with a miniature glass angel from the table centre-piece and she imagined those fingers toying with her—

Stop. Now.

He wasn't here for her pleasure; he was here to see Brie and share Christmas.

Olivia's family had always celebrated the day at home, with a tree and silly hats and enough food to feed an entire naval fleet. Even last year after her mother had passed away, she'd ensured they had a traditional day—her and Brie and a couple of single girlfriends from the health centre where they worked.

'Are you into natural beauty therapy like Breanna?' Jett asked, glancing at Brie as she sauntered back to resume her seat at the table.

'I work in the field of natural medicine. I share a suite of rooms with Brie, a massage therapist and a kinesiologist. I've taken a month's leave to participate in the race and focus on our fundraising.'

'Livvie has an advanced diploma in Naturopathy,' Brie boasted before Olivia could get another word out. 'She's also got a degree in Health Science. Now she's halfway through a business course so she can set up a cancer retreat. *And* there's her charity foundation, and—'

'*Brie...*' Olivia felt herself flush at Brie's enthusiasm.

She'd learned that guys weren't interested in a woman whose academic achievements outstripped theirs. It had never bothered her before. It shouldn't bother her now, but, for some reason she couldn't figure out, it did. She wanted Jett to see her first and foremost as a woman. Which made no sense at all.

'…And we're going to be business partners when the centre's up and running.' Smiling, Brie sat back and crossed her arms.

Jett regarded Olivia a moment, thoughtful. 'Are you going to fill me in on your charity? Does it have a name?'

'You mean she hasn't told you?' Brie's voice rose in astonishment.

'We didn't get around to it,' he said, eyes still on Olivia.

'That must be a first.' Brie laughed. 'She lives to talk about her Pink Snowflake Foundation. Jett, you must be the only one she hasn't harassed—and I do mean that in the nicest possible way.' When Olivia turned, Brie's eyes were twinkling at her across the table.

Brie was right. Olivia had been so infatuated with Jett last night, she'd forgotten to talk his ear off about her work and convince him to contribute. 'My mother died of breast cancer and I'm working on building a retreat for cancer survivors and those undergoing therapy to recuperate. It's still not much more than a very expensive dream but we'll get there eventually. Mum and I set up the foundation five years ago after she got sick the first time.'

'She has an amazing vision,' Brie said. 'And I'm proud to say I'm going to be a part of it. *After* I survive the race.'

'That's the positive attitude I want to hear.' But Olivia's grin quickly sobered. She was honouring a pact she and her mum had made years ago—to race their yacht in the Sydney to Hobart. Not just in memory of her mother, but all the women in her family who'd died of breast cancer. All women with breast cancer.

'This time tomorrow we'll be heading down the New South Wales coast.' Excitement and nerves were building and tangling in her stomach.

'What's the name of the boat you're sailing on?' Jett leaned back as the wait staff appeared to whisk away the plates.

'Yacht,' Olivia corrected. '*Chasing Dawn*. She may be small but she's a real and classic beauty.' They'd bought the old sea-craft together when her mum had been in remission and there'd been hope.

His gaze flicked between them. 'So two females on the crew. Doesn't that bring some sort of bad luck—women and boats?'

Oh, for goodness' sake. 'What about Aussie Jessica Watson's record-breaking solo sail around the world at sixteen? And *did you know* that the only yacht to reach Hobart in 1946 was skippered by the first *woman* ever to take part? Would you call that *bad luck*?'

'Your skipper obviously doesn't mind the distraction,' he went on, as if Olivia hadn't spoken. 'Does he ever get a little too up-close-and-*nautical* with his crew?'

The way he said that…in an entirely sexual way…made her want to slap him.

She should have expected it: the cocky grin, the sexual spark in his eyes. His sheer masculine arrogance. And to think they'd been having an almost pleasant conversation moments ago. She kept her cool, took a long, calming swallow of iced water. 'Not at all. Everyone concentrates on their job. No one gets distracted.'

He raised his brows. 'I bet.'

'There are no *nauticals* on our yacht, *Mr* Davies. We're a team—we work as a team, everyone's equal.'

'I'd like to see that.'

How he'd meant it was anyone's guess but Olivia was inclined to think it wasn't in a flattering non-gender-biased way. 'Would you really?' She snipped the words as if she were dead-heading roses. 'I can easily accommodate you there.'

He grinned, even white teeth flashing like a toothpaste ad, anticipation in his eyes. 'Yeah? You going to invite me aboard?'

'Yeah.' A plan was coming together in her head and she felt a grin to rival his spread over her face. 'One of our crew had to pull out due to illness three days ago. And you would be the perfect person to fill the void. Snowflake needs publicity. A quick word to the media and you'd be doing me, us—my *foundation*—a huge, huge favour. Wouldn't he, Brie?'

She glanced at Brie, who'd not said a word but seemed to be enjoying the moment as much as Olivia. 'Yes,' she said, slowly. 'I reckon you're right.'

When Olivia looked back at Jett, she noticed a little of his smugness had slipped.

'On the boat?'

'*Yacht*. You'd love it, Jett.' Olivia lowered her voice an octave and added a husky purr. 'The entire crew is female. Imagine. All those bronzed beauties in bikinis.' Except they wouldn't be in bikinis, but the word image begged to be painted for him all the same. 'And I'm sure you'd enjoy hot-bunking.'

His eyes grew round, his brows raised. 'Hot-bunking?'

She nodded. 'You'll find out if you join us.'

'The entire crew? The skipper too?' His smugness seemed to have disappeared altogether.

She tipped an imaginary cap. 'Yours truly.'

'But…'

'I know. Unlucky for some, but *Chasing Dawn*'s had her fair share of women aboard and she's not sprung a leak yet.' She swore he blanched and she pressed her lips together to stop her enjoyment from showing too much. 'Come on, Jett. Say yes. Please. We need you.'

'Please, Jett,' Brie chimed in. 'It's for a good cause and we're having roast quail and veg on our first night at sea.'

Olivia knew they'd never win the race—it had never been about winning. The whole reason behind the motivation was to raise money and awareness, and a celebrity aboard would be just what they needed. A sexy celebrity chef even better.

A sexy celebrity chef out of his comfort zone the best of all—the media would *eat* it up.

Roast quail. Was that supposed to be a deal maker? Jett detected the tiniest twitch at the corner of Olivia's mouth and ground down on his back teeth. He'd been outmanoeuvred. His masculine pride was at stake, because he knew from bitter personal experience that seasickness could turn the toughest of the tough into a whimpering shipwreck of a man.

And that was before leaving the dock.

'You're right about the late notice. Too bad, I didn't bring the appropriate gear.'

'No worries.' Her reassuring tone did nothing to alleviate his quickly burgeoning discomfort. Already he could feel the roll and swell beneath his feet.

'We have caps and T-shirts with the foundation's logo left over from last year's charity run,' she told him. 'Rest assured, we'll find one to fit you. And we have abundant spray jackets and oilskins on hand for when it gets rough.'

When it gets rough. Her gaze drifted down his body as she spoke, raising goose-bumps and questions he wasn't game to ask. Like whether it was too late to check in. Or back out. Except quitting was never going to be an option.

'Think about it over dessert,' Brie suggested, giving him

time to digest this new twist as a traditional flaming plum pudding was carried in and set on the table.

He helped himself to a second slice a few moments later. Olivia surprised him. Her drive and enthusiasm for a cause she believed in. Other girls her age were self-absorbed party princesses. When he'd first seen her he'd thought she was the same, but now he knew differently. And he wanted to help her.

But did it have to be on a boat?

He was still digesting the idea when they'd scraped their bowls clean, licked the last of the brandy sauce from their spoons and Breanna said, 'Presents time,' and pushed up from the table.

An uncomfortable sensation slid down Jett's spine but Breanna was right behind him, her hands on his shoulders. 'Relax, bro.'

Slipping a hand around his arm, she steered him to the Christmas tree with its glossy wrapped parcels beneath.

He reached for the swing bag with its exclusive store logo etched in silver. 'This is for you.' He held it out to Brie. 'It's probably not the right sort for a beauty therapist...' He shrugged, feeling awkward.

She grinned. 'French label, are you kidding? I'll love it. Thank you.'

He turned to Olivia. 'I wasn't expecting you.' He realised he meant that in more ways than one as he handed her the tissue-wrapped crystal vase he'd purchased in the hotel's gift shop earlier this morning.

She met his gaze with a smile in her eyes that said she was as surprised as he. That maybe she'd forgiven him for the moment. 'It was all kind of last minute, wasn't it?'

'I've waited a long time to share Christmas with you,' Breanna said. 'So here you are.' She reached down, picked up a box, held it out. 'Merry Christmas.'

He took it from her hands but it felt weird. 'Thanks.'

'Merry Christmas, Jett.' Olivia held out a smaller packet.

'Hey, I didn't expect—'

'Why don't you sit on the couch and open them?' Breanna suggested, sitting down herself and patting the space beside her, then reaching into her swing bag. 'I can't wait to smell this perfume.'

He sat next to his sister. Since it was on top, he opened Olivia's gift first. A pair of soft kid gloves.

'For Melbourne's winter,' she told him. 'I hear it gets cold there.'

'Thanks. They're great.' He admired the deep charcoal colour, her thoughtfulness. 'You've never been to Melbourne, then?'

'Never got around to it.'

'Less than an hour's flight from Hobart?' He glanced at her, surprised, and caught a wistfulness in her eyes before she blinked it away.

'Never seem to get time to travel these days.'

'You'll have to visit some time. You'd love the boutique shopping. I—'

'Shopping's not one of my priorities.' Her voice was brisk. 'At least not the indulgent kind of shopping you're referring to.'

'You'd enjoy it anyway,' he assured her, turning his attention to Breanna's gift. He lifted the lid on the box. Inside was a home-made Christmas cake. The enticing aroma of brandied fruit filled his nostrils.

He nodded and said, 'Family recipe?' then wished he hadn't.

'No. One of your tropical fruit specialties, actually.' She rose and walked to the tree and picked up another box. 'One more.'

'Breanna. You shouldn't have.' Damn, he really meant

it. She had no idea how uncomfortable she made him feel, and with Olivia watching on, he just wanted to walk out and leave the pair of them to their sentimental traditions.

Beneath the wrapping paper he found a beautifully bound album. Old leather. The kind that might have been a photograph album a long time ago. Its pages were empty. 'What's this for?'

'I thought maybe if you had some old photos, you could put them in here with some of mine around the same time period. A kind of combined effort. And I'm hoping that we're going to make some memories together to fill the latter pages.'

'I don't have any photos.' Photos were memories and he didn't want them. He didn't do sentimental and nostalgia. Especially not for Christmas. 'Excuse me, I've remembered I've got to make a couple of business calls.' Pushing up, he strode to the door.

'Where are you going?' Olivia's voice. 'What about tomorrow? Are you in or out?'

He didn't turn around. 'Later.'

CHAPTER FIVE

'THAT DIDN'T GO so well.' Brie grabbed up a cushion and hugged it close. 'The album idea was a mistake. I didn't expect him to react that way.'

'Not a mistake. He's a chef—unpredictable—need we say more?' But Olivia didn't know his past so how could she judge? But business calls on Christmas Day? 'Give him time, Brie.' She sat next to her, smoothing the torn wrapping paper over her lap as she spoke. 'Why don't you give your sexy skipper a call and tell him you're cleared for the rest of the afternoon? He's single with an all-male crew, right? He'd probably love a bit of female company.'

Brie was slow in smiling but she unfolded herself and stood. 'I might just do that. If you're sure.'

'Of course I am. I'm going to check on our ride for tomorrow, make sure everything's okay, take a stroll around the harbour while I'm out.' Anything to soothe tomorrow's nervous anticipation. 'See you later.'

An hour later Olivia walked downstairs on her way to the marina, going over last-minute details in her head. And Jett's disappearance. This evening was the last chance for him and his sister to catch up before the race, and he'd walked out on her.

Following a hunch, she detoured via the bar and *bingo*—

she saw Jett propped on a bar stool, a beer in his hands. Chatting up the long tall brunette beside him who looked as if she'd been poured into her shimmery red sheath. Reindeer antlers bobbed on her head as she talked and smiled and pushed her boobs into his personal space.

She counted herself lucky she and Jett hadn't taken things further and watched the pair of them. On closer inspection, she noticed the brunette seemed to be doing most of the talking.

The woman he *should* have been talking with was Brie, but no. It just demonstrated oh-so-clearly that was how men were and why she didn't waste her time with them.

Like her father's decision to leave when Mum had got sick. Easier to walk away than to face the tough times. Like Brie's dad—Jett's father—who'd walked away from a child he'd made.

Jason who'd walked away because he didn't like her sexual inexperience.

Maybe Jett felt her silent criticism because he turned and looked right at her. *Déjà vu.* Last night all over again, except this time Olivia was ready for the delicious onslaught. She wouldn't be seduced a second time.

He slid off the stool without so much as a glance back at the woman he'd been talking with and headed Olivia's way. Her jaw firmed as painful memories scratched over old scars. Like father like son. Olivia's father hadn't looked back either.

She watched the confident way he approached her, his long strides closing the gap between them, an almost-lift at one corner of his mouth. As if this afternoon hadn't happened and he was ready to continue with Olivia where they'd left off last night.

She lifted both hands waist high, palms out in front of her.

'I want to talk to you,' she told him crisply across a couple or so metres of floor space.

'Olivia. Nice name, by the way. We never got as far as introducing ourselves last night.'

His voice was casual but when he reached her she realised he wasn't ready to carry her off and have his way with her after all. He had the attitude down pat, but the darker, almost distant glint in his already dark eyes told a different story. 'Can I buy you a drink?'

'What about your lady friend?' Olivia jutted her chin towards the bar.

'She's not with me. I was being polite.'

Frustration seethed in her blood and her voice gathered strength as it rose. 'You want to talk about polite?'

He took her arm, turned her around and steered her towards the door. 'Why don't we walk while we talk—unless you want an audience?'

'Fine. I'm headed to the marina to check on our yacht.' Then because she remembered telling Brie to give Jett time only an hour earlier, she injected a composure she didn't feel into her voice and asked, 'Would you care to join me?'

They hit the crowded, sun-baked footpath. Jett might have only just met Olivia but he'd known she'd hunt him down. He knew what she was going to say too, because he had to admit he'd been a bit of an ass. He was going to have to smooth things over.

Which was fine with him because he wanted to indulge his eyes awhile and see her again. He flicked his eyes her way and watched the sun tangle in her hair, setting it on fire. To breathe in that uniquely fragrant combination of warm and cool. To—

'Did you have to be so rude to Brie? That album idea meant a lot. What the hell's wrong with you?'

—And to watch the spark come alive while she told him what she thought of him.

He liked that spark. It seemed to light her from the inside and grew brighter with passion. It made him want to grab her right here, right now, and kiss the hell out of her and see if he couldn't steal a little of that light for himself. 'I'll talk to Breanna. Explain.'

'I hope so.'

As close as siblings, he thought. A childhood memory flitted darkly through his mind. His father telling Jett he couldn't live with him because Breanna had taken his place. 'Your loyalty's touching.'

'And your cynicism's showing.'

'Guess it is.' He lengthened his stride so that she had to hurry to keep up.

'Don't you understand loyalty?'

'Never had a reason to.' He understood independence and self-sufficiency. Responsibility and achievement. He answered to no one and he liked it that way.

'What about your staff?'

He frowned. 'What about them?'

'Don't you appreciate their loyalty?'

'I don't have staff. Not long term.'

'I wonder why,' she muttered almost to herself.

'Because I'm not in one place long enough.'

'What about friends? Or don't you have them either.' It wasn't a question.

'I have acquaintances. No point making friends.'

She stared at him, obviously missing his logic. 'Brie's not just a friend,' she pointed out. 'She's your sister. Blood. *Family*.'

Her impassioned words unsettled him. 'In the New Year. I'll work on it. Satisfied?'

'Guess I'll have to be.'

'Hey, it's Christmas, how about a truce?'

She skirted around a kid trying out his brand-new skateboard. 'Okay, truce. For now. I don't want your last night with Brie spoiled by our inability to understand one another.'

'So where is she?'

'Spending time with a guy since you walked out on her. She'll be back later.' They'd reached the marina where the yachts were moored. 'Let's talk about yachts instead,' she said, and stepped out of her shoes. 'Ever sailed in one of these?'

'Took the *Spirit of Tasmania* across Bass Strait once.' He spoke of the passenger and freight vessel linking Tasmania to the mainland.

'Enjoy it?'

He rubbed the heel of his hand over his belly in wretched remembrance. 'Even with a deluxe cabin it was eleven hours of pure hell.'

She nodded, swinging her shoes at her side. 'Bass Strait can get pretty rough.'

He didn't tell her they'd had smooth seas for the whole voyage. That he was no sailor in any way, shape or form.

They passed several magnificent craft while Olivia described each one in pretty impressive detail.

Then he saw *Chasing Dawn* bobbing gently on the water and his throat went dry. Was he actually considering—even remotely—going to sea in this child's bath toy?

She interpreted his expression correctly. 'She may be small but she's proud and every last inch of her is seaworthy.' On light feet, she almost skipped ahead and waved a hand towards it when he reached her. 'Come aboard.'

He gestured. 'After you.'

The deck tilted ever so slightly beneath him as he stepped on board behind her. He had an impression of ropes and canvas and an animated Olivia amidst the chaos.

'You're the first male to be invited aboard, so welcome. I hope that's not a bad omen.'

Making reference to his earlier gaff about women and boats. Should've kept his mouth shut.

'So do I.' He could tell she was determined to impress him with her baby. So far *not* good. 'Where's the rest of the boat?' he wanted to know, glancing at the end only a few metres away. Or was it called the stern? He was out of his depth.

'Down here...' Then she was descending through the hatch, leaving him to follow.

Humid, stuffy air met his nostrils.

He took in the surroundings—it didn't take long. What was virtually a narrow tube of polished wood, glimpses of laminate and aluminium. A few envelope-sized windows. Claustrophobic was an apt description. So much for any ideas about getting *nautical*. 'Do I get the grand tour?'

Olivia smiled, pride warming her all the way through. 'Of course.' A few moments later—because it really didn't take long to tour the *Chasing Dawn*—Olivia pulled two bottles of mineral water from the fridge. 'Have a seat.' She set them on the tiny table between them, unscrewed hers and raised it. 'Cheers.'

He did the same and they both drank.

Olivia hadn't realised how small and cramped the vessel was until Jett had come aboard. How he seemed to have sucked all the oxygen from the air. How his skin looked more swarthy down here, the stubble thicker, blacker. He reminded her of a romantic version of a pirate. Except she doubted even imaginary pirates smelled this good; his suave woodsy cologne enticed her to breathe more deeply.

'You're planning roast quail tomorrow night.' He gestured to below decks with his bottle. 'Here?'

Even his voice sounded too rich for the space. It seemed to reverberate across the short distance between them and brush up against her chest like a hand. 'That's what the microwave's for,' she said. 'Something special for our first night at sea.' She gave him a wry smile. 'Don't worry, I'm not cooking; I've had it specially prepared.'

'The skipper, eh.' He cast another look around the cabin. 'You're an experienced sailor, then.'

'My parents were dedicated yachts-people. I've sailed all my life.' She tilted the bottle towards him. 'You're safe with me.'

He glanced around them again. 'Safe from pirates?' He lowered his voice to a conspiratorial murmur and she leaned closer almost without thought.

'Pirates,' she joked. 'Off the coast of Tasmania. With helicopters and the press following our voyage?'

'Yeah. Captain Jack Sparrow and company. Ever see any?'

There'd been a time off Madagascar, she recalled, and rubbed the sudden shiver from her arms. 'They're bloody and vicious and these days they use rocket propelled grenades and automatic rifles rather than the cannon and cutlass.'

'You don't find the notion of pirates romantic, then.' He sounded almost disappointed.

'Not in the least,' she decided, brushing off her romantic vision of a piratical Jett. 'So you can forget any pirate ways and whatever else you may have had in mind.' She checked the time. 'We'd better get going.'

'Not yet. First we should discuss this attraction.'

Olivia almost choked on her water.

'This crazy thing between us,' he went on. 'It could be awkward—best friends and brother.'

'Very awkward. So we'll put last night behind us. Forget it.' Heat rose up her neck and into her cheeks and she glared at him, forced herself to hold his gaze. 'We don't need—'

'I've heard the sound you make when you come. That soft bitey noise between a sigh and a scream.'

Oh. My. God. 'I did *not*—'

'But you did.' His eyes crinkled, that delicious-looking mouth tilted up at the corners. 'What's more, I want to hear it again. You don't think we should discuss it?'

She tipped her bottle to her lips, gulped as if she were dying of dehydration then cleared her throat. 'Since a *discussion* involves two or more people, will you let me finish a sentence at least?' When he cocked his head to one side, she firmed her chin and said, 'We've acknowledged it and now we move on.'

'I've acknowledged it. I'm not so sure about you,' he said, tilting his bottle at her.

'Okay. Yes. I acknowledge it. Satisfied?'

'Not nearly.' But his eyes twinkled, his lips twitched. 'We need to get it out of the way if we're going to be in such close quarters for the next few days.'

Her heart leapt into her throat then took a giant tumble. 'You're coming with us?'

'Isn't that what you want?'

'No—yes… Um…'

'You've changed your mind?'

'No. No. Not at all. Brie'll be thrilled.'

'Not you?'

'Of course. I'm happy too. Very happy. For Brie's sake. And thank you,' she finished.

'Okay, I can live with that.' Jett didn't think he'd enjoyed anything more in a long time than watching a twitchy Olivia blush and stammer. It was almost worth taking this marine misadventure just to see her lost for words.

Almost.

She pushed her hair off her face, seemed to regain her composure and said, 'You'd better get a good night's rest, then, because you'll need to familiarise yourself with the safety aspect before we leave. We need Brie.' She tapped her phone. 'Brie? I need you down at the marina asap.' She smiled at something Breanna said. 'Jett's decided to join us.' Pause. 'No, I didn't talk him into it. Okay, see you…um… how long do you think you'll be?' Pause. 'Okay.'

She disconnected and pushed up. 'Brie's on her way. We rise at four a.m., race starts at one. I've got stuff to do.'

'Wait just a damn minute. We still haven't had our discussion.'

'I don't think we—'

'Neither do I, Trouble, but here we are.' If he was going to die at sea, he wanted to make sure it was worth it. He pushed up as well and stepped into her path at the edge of the table, and their bodies bumped.

He felt her breasts rise against his chest as she sucked in a breath and stared up at him. It wasn't the only body part rising—and she knew that too.

The sea lapped softly against the hull and cast the late afternoon's watery reflections across the boat's interior, bathing them both in a blinding crimson glow.

She didn't step back, nor did she encourage him. She simply continued watching him, expressionless but for the spark of heated arousal in her eyes that gave her away.

'I want you to think about this…' Contemplating, he slid his index finger along the top of her dress, his gaze following the freckled swells and the valley between.

She shifted restlessly against him. 'We can't…'

'So tell me to stop.' He lowered his head to nuzzle. Just a nip on that tender spot between shoulder and neck, a lingering taste where her fragrance bloomed with the heat of her skin.

She arched her neck, giving him better access, and murmured, 'St-o-p.'

'I'll stop when you mean it.' Sweeping her hair aside, he cruised his lips from the side of her neck to beneath her jaw to a neat little ear lobe. Greedy little bites that only whetted his appetite for more. 'You taste incredible.' He nibbled along her jawbone. 'I want to taste you all over,' he murmured and was rewarded with a little shiver. 'But I'm prepared to stop at a kiss.'

She didn't answer, obviously too turned on by his moves to speak.

'For now,' he finished. He smoothed her hair again, loving its silky feel and fascinated with the way the light played over its vibrant strands, turning them golden. He straightened and watched her face, animated with conflicting emotions.

'Jett, it won't make a scrap of difference.' She watched him, her chin firm, her eyes resolute. 'This race is too important on so many levels. I can't be distracted…'

He smiled and her almost appalled gaze dropped to his mouth. Banding his arms around her waist, he pulled her closer, explored the shell of her ear with his tongue and whispered, 'Wrong.'

She pushed at his chest. 'No, I—' He cut off her excuses with a kiss that started out to prove a point and quickly turned into something more.

Her mouth yielded and opened beneath his and he took instant advantage of the honeyed heat within, sliding his tongue against hers in a dance, a duel or a demand—he didn't know which. He didn't care. She was a feisty combination of strength and vulnerability, of seduction and naïvety, and he found her completely enchanting.

She didn't try to push him away again, nor did she reach for him, but the fury of her heartbeat thundering against his as their upper bodies touched was the answer he was looking for.

Gathering her loosely flowing hair, he wound it around both fists and tugged her head back the better to taste her. If he was looking for surrender, he didn't find it with Olivia. She met him will for will. Force for force. Passion for passion.

He could have her in that *aft berth* as she called it, in five seconds flat—she wouldn't refuse him and it would be fast and furious and mutually satisfying—but even in his lust-crazed state, he knew it would also be a mistake.

Breanna was on her way and there wasn't nearly enough time to do what he wanted to do.

With a good deal of reluctance and admirable restraint, he lifted his lips and drew back slowly, watching her. Huge glassy eyes watched him back. He was surprised to find himself as breathless as she. 'After the race, Trouble,' he promised, letting her hair slide through his fingers as he stepped away, 'we're going to finish this.'

She gave him no indication how she felt about his decision. Footsteps approaching had them drawing further apart. Olivia patted at her hair while Jett resumed his seat at the table for obvious reasons.

'Brie.' Olivia darted towards her as if she couldn't wait to get away. 'I've got a million things to do, so I'll leave Jett with you.'

She turned to him, not quite meeting his gaze, residual heat in her eyes, her cheeks a little too pink, her movements a little too jerky.

'I'll be attending a weather briefing in the morning so I won't see you till you board,' she told him. 'But Brie'll go over the safety procedures. She'll look after you, fill you in with what you need, get you up to speed until it's time to leave. The rest of your gear can go with ours; it'll be in Hobart when we arrive.'

Look after you? Screw that. He aimed a killer smile at her, just to watch that spark come to life again. 'Looking forward to it.'

CHAPTER SIX

SYDNEY HARBOUR'S DEEP blue was awash with vessels of every size and shape, ferrying binocular-wielding spectators. Pleasure craft bobbed on the water from a safe distance; colourful sails billowed in the stiff breeze.

Without a specific role other than to sit in a designated spot and 'look sexy for the cameras', Jett used the lead-up time to appreciate *Chasing Dawn*'s all-female crew as they went about their assigned tasks. He barely felt the rocking movement beneath his feet, refused to acknowledge the tiny curl of unease beneath his breastbone.

He found the helicopter-circling media's up-close and personal interest in the Jettsetter Chef over the top. He shrugged, uncomfortable in the neon-candy-pink T-shirt and cap, and gave a double thumbs-up to a TV crew above them. It was for a worthwhile cause, and their crew's flirtatious glances, the gentle teasing and admiration for his support made up for it.

All the crew, that was, except for their preoccupied skipper, who obviously had more important matters on her mind.

A monster yacht cruised by, its deck crawling with male-model types standing around looking like a shoot for a men's magazine.

If he had to be on a boat, this was the one to be on. In this case, size did not matter. Surrounded by super-fit, sun-bronzed beauties who'd each dropped by—Miranda, Flo and Samantha—and extended a personal invitation to show him the sights and tastes of Tassie. Samantha, the blue-eyed blonde, had explained how the six-person crew had been divided into watches called Wet and Wild. She'd told him he was on the Wild watch with her and Brie. She'd kind of winked when she'd said it.

He forced himself to relax and watched the action around him, cleavage, perfume, feminine voices. He loved women—loved their curves and silky skin, their scents and tastes. The way they insinuated themselves against him and made him feel like a king for however long it lasted—one night, a week. A month at most.

Five-minute warning shot. Twelve-knot breeze on the harbour. A gusty change expected later this evening.

The crew were in their positions. From his spot he got a glimpse of Olivia, her hair tucked beneath her cap, looking gloriously intense in her skimpy pink T-shirt that rode up at the back, giving him a tantalising view of flesh as she moved lightly across the deck. Her toned and tanned legs flashed in the sun and her feet were bare. He decided there was nothing sexier than a bare-footed skipper.

She'd offered him prescription-strength seasickness medication, which he'd waved away. He didn't tell her he'd purchased an over-the-counter generic brand from a nearby pharmacy last night. Apart from that time, he'd hardly laid eyes on her since that kiss in the galley late yesterday afternoon.

An urgent commotion broke out amongst the crew, catching his attention. He heard the words 'main power' and 'power winch' and a few sailor-worthy curses.

He half rose but he caught sight of Breanna sprinting across the deck already shaking her head as if she expected him to offer his expertise. 'Olivia knows what she's doing.'

Of course she did. Obviously a boat mechanic on top of everything else. Since he didn't have a clue about boat mechanics and he'd only be in the way in addition to showcasing his *lack* of expertise, he leaned back again and watched the crew work feverishly to fix whatever the problem was.

And it would be fixed, he had no doubt. Wonder Woman was in charge. Interesting. He'd never been remotely involved with a take-charge woman.

The girls returned to their positions, problem obviously sorted. Seconds later the starter pistol cracked the air and they were off, tacking against the north-easterly wind. As they rounded the marker outside Sydney Heads, the huge and distinctive pink spinnaker sail unfurled, accelerating them to a fast rate of knots in a southerly direction down the coast.

Smooth sailing on a sparkling blue sea, fresh sea air. Roast quail and veg for dinner tonight. A single male in a boatful of gorgeous girls.

They settled in, the rhythmic motion almost hypnotic, and his mind wandered. He envied Olivia her focus and drive and dedication. She had her plan, she'd charted a path for her life and nothing was going to divert her from it.

Whereas he was drifting. Career-wise he'd been restless and unsettled for a while. He needed a change of direction, something to bring back the zing in life, to motivate him. Even if it had nothing to do with career, this sailing-cum-fundraising opportunity was a new experience. He gazed at the tilting horizon. Out here on the endless Pacific Ocean he felt as if he was on the brink of something new, different, exciting.

He'd not felt so alive in a long time.

He wished he were dead.

On deck and huddled into a spray jacket over his hoodie, Jett stared listlessly at the night's stormy horizon lifting and sinking, up, down… Death was preferable to this washing machine on spin cycle. He swallowed several times as bile rose up his throat. Again. His quail dinner and worse—his pride—had disappeared overboard in spectacular fashion even before the change in weather had really shaken things up. He'd woken for his Wild watch and emerged from the sticky fume-filled cabin and into the fresh sea air and *bam*.

The watch was nearly over. Thirty more minutes. Then all he wanted was to be left alone to die in peace. A familiar figure emerged from below decks and began making her way towards him in the dimness. The sexy skipper. A hot tide of humiliation washed through him and he averted his eyes to the clouds scudding across the night sky. Neither wish was going to be granted, it seemed.

'I can take over here.' The voice of his mistletoe angel, barely audible in the bluster. Offering him the chance to slip into her still-warm bunk—the mysterious hot-bunking, she'd lured him in with—and grant his last wishes after all.

'I'm fine.' He huddled deeper into his hoodie, pulled it low over his sweat-damp brow to hide his malaise. 'Go away, it's not time yet.'

Unfazed by his curt demand, she sat down beside him. 'The weather's starting to ease up.'

He leaned away, super-aware that his Armani aftershave had been replaced by infinitely more unpleasant and pungent odours, and popped a peppermint in his mouth. 'Could've fooled me.'

'You're doing great, Jett.'

Her tone wasn't sympathetic, just matter-of-fact with an injection of humour. Even in his misery, he appreciated that. 'Glad the skipper thinks so.' He kept his gaze down, alongside him, and saw that her long legs were tightly encased in denim but those sexy feet of hers were still bare. If he could just be sure he wasn't going to spew in front of her…

He pressed his lips together. He didn't think he could ever face her again if that happened.

'Talking takes your mind off the queasiness.'

'Yeah, right.'

'Okay, go ahead, ask me something.'

'Why bare feet?'

She wiggled her toes like a kid in sand. 'For the grip when the deck's slippery. And bare toes can twist around ropes—I'm pretty good at that.'

Jeez, chirpy as a seagull with a hot chip. 'You're pretty good at a lot of things nautical.'

'I lived on-board a cruiser until I went to high school.'

He forgot his reluctance to look her in the eye and stared at her. 'Yeah?'

She laughed, a joyous sound, her face aglow even in the grey night. 'It was a large cruiser. I was an only child and my parents home-schooled me while we travelled the world. They called it a living education.'

'A fair description, I suppose.'

'Yes.' She pushed back her hood and smoothed her hair from her face and he realised the wind had lessened. 'But when I reached secondary-school age and my mum's sister was diagnosed with cancer, they sold the cruiser and bought a property out of Hobart to be near her.' She chuckled. 'High school was a learning curve for me; I'd never been around kids my own age before.'

She'd learned to be content with her own company. A bit like him, in a random kind of way. His gaze lifted and he saw a break in the clouds—he'd been so preoccupied he'd not noticed. 'When did your mother pass away?'

'Eighteen months ago.'

'What about your dad, does—?'

'I haven't seen or heard from him in years. He walked out on us when Mum got sick the first time.' She spoke without the emotion he read in her eyes, the dip he saw in her shoulders. 'She was in remission when we bought *Chasing Dawn* together. We had hope then, that she'd make it, and we set up Snowflake, but her condition deteriorated sooner than we expected.'

'You mentioned your aunt. Did she…?'

'Breast cancer runs in my family. My grandmother, my cousin, and great-grandmother too, they suspect.' She spoke matter-of-factly, her eyes on middle distance. Avoiding his.

He frowned. The familial link to the disease would surely be a concern for her, but she didn't elaborate and he didn't want to broach a delicate subject. 'Why a pink snowflake?'

'When individual ice crystals bump into others they grow into the stunning and unique shape of a snowflake. We think of ourselves as those individuals working together to create something worthwhile and beautiful. Pink because it's raising awareness for women's cancers.'

He looked up at the sky where a few stars peeked through and thought about what she'd said. How she'd turned something bad into something good. 'That's pretty special.' He admired her for it. It also made him question his own life's contributions—pretty damn ordinary.

'I like to think so,' she said on a note of cheer. 'Thank you again for sailing with us and helping make a difference.'

'I've not done much.' Except chuck all over your lovingly polished deck.

'Oh, but you have,' she reassured him with abundant enthusiasm. 'You've drawn attention to our foundation just by being here. I expect a huge influx of donations and sponsorships.' Her grin was full of fun. 'You can keep the T-shirt and cap as a thank-you.'

She turned to him at the same time he turned to look at her. She was sharing the humour, her eyes sparkling in the night's soft grey light, her bound hair coming adrift from its plait, tendrils spiralling behind her into the wind.

And there it was again. That flare of attraction. Hot, bright, bewitching. Reciprocated.

Despite his roiling stomach, lust smouldered along his veins. With her torso covered in a padded jacket, Jett's focus narrowed to her smiling lips—lusciously plump and unglossed.

They were still smiling when she said, 'Your support means a lot to Brie too when clearly sailing's not your thing.'

Nothing like mention of his sister and seasickness to douse the lust sparks. He raked fingers over his skull, discovered his hands were disgustingly shaky, like his gut. What the hell had he been thinking, telling her they were going to finish...whatever this thing was between them? He'd be lucky to get past the starting line. She valued commitment, loyalty. Stickability. Her focus and her priority were with other people.

He was a travelling one-man show.

She'd been trouble from that first glimpse. Trouble from that first kiss. Trouble from that first glide of his hand over silken female flesh.

Trouble.

So why the *hell* was he hung up on her?

'Leave you to it,' he muttered, pushing up and listing to one side as the boat pitched and rolled.

'Jett. Caref—'

'I'm f—' His stomach revolted and he waved her away, hauled himself to the railing and retched pitifully over the side.

Humiliation complete.

CHAPTER SEVEN

SINCE THEY WERE on different watches and Olivia was occupied with duties that included keeping them on course, she didn't see much of Jett. Still, there were four other women more than eager to see to his welfare. Cater to his every whim. In his current state of malaise she was pretty sure they were safe from his unique brand of charm. He was, to all intents and purposes, harmless.

On the following morning when she forced her gritty eyes open after a fitful two-hour doze, she heard the sounds of feminine laughter and Jett's low, husky rumble in the thick of it. Obviously seasickness was no longer such an issue.

She checked the time, pushed up, eyes narrowing as Miranda's laugh echoed with his. A mouth-watering aroma teased her nostrils as she reached the galley and her stomach gurgled.

The threesome were relaxed around the tiny table, sharing some joke she hadn't heard. The chick magnet working his irresistible charm.

Not so harmless.

Downright sexy, in fact, with one of the heavy vinyl aprons they used aboard moulded tight over his broad chest making him look disgustingly virile and domesticated at the same time.

He didn't notice her standing there practically salivating

until she said, 'Jett, I hate to spoil the party but isn't it your watch?' She lied—she didn't hate it at all.

Miranda and Flo paused at her no-nonsense tone, fluffy white scones with lashings of jam and cream halfway to their mouths. Flo looked apologetically flustered, straightened and pushed back from the table. 'Livvie, Brie said—'

'Breanna and Sam have it covered upstairs,' Jett told Olivia smoothly, staying right where he was and reaching for his bottle of ginger ale. 'My sister put me to work. Come and try them while they're hot, skipper. I was just going to see if you were awake and bring you a couple...'

Yeah, right. 'Let me guess, you were distracted.'

He shot her a raised-brow look, chugged back on his bottle.

'They're so-o good,' Miranda groaned, licking cream from her lips. 'I didn't know microwaved scones could turn out so delicious. Thanks, Jett,' she said in a wily feminine voice Olivia had never heard her use. She rose—reluctantly, Olivia noted—placing a few scones in a shallow plastic bowl and exchanging looks with Flo. 'Let's take some up for the others. You two stay here and relax.'

'So you're feeling lots better, then?' Olivia enquired sweetly after the girls had gone.

'Getting my sea legs,' he said. 'Isn't that what you call it?' But his complexion still had a greenish tinge and dark smudges lay beneath his eyes. 'The girls were complaining about the lack of comfort food on board.'

He wasn't eating, she noticed, and a twinge of sympathy stirred her enough to say, 'You didn't have to cook. Don't let *the girls* take advantage.'

He stood, cleared the crumbs from the table. 'And here I was expecting you to tell me off for taking advantage of *them.*'

Her lips twitched. 'Were you?'

He shot her a glance. 'There's only one girl I'm interested in on this boat.'

Her blood quickened through her veins. 'Yacht.'

'Whatever. Don't be shy.' When she just stared at him, he indicated the plate on the table with a jerk of his chin while he rinsed the utensils in the tiny sink.

Oh. Of course. She helped herself and bit in. They tasted like heaven. 'And you made them in that itty-bitty microwave?' The mystery was, *how*?

'Yep.' He moved to the pantry and began pulling out her basic supply of ingredients. 'I'm going to show you how to make simple muffins so next time you take this itty-bitty boat out, you can have some comfort food for the crew.'

Just her and him, in this itty-bitty space. She remembered too well the last time they'd been here. The way he'd kissed her. The way she'd responded. 'Oh. No, I—'

'We're both off duty.' He set the mixing bowl on the table, shook in flour. 'Would you rather put the time to a different kind of use?' His eyes burned into hers, turning her blood to syrup. 'Your choice.'

She looked away fast, reached for the spice rack. 'Okay, muffins.'

He held out the other vinyl apron. 'I'll mix the batter while I tell you how to make a perfect streusel topping.'

As instructed, she added the brown sugar, chopped nuts and spices to her bowl while he beat eggs and stirred them into the dry mix he'd prepared.

'Who taught you to cook?' she asked to distract her thoughts away from imagining him whipping the mix in *only* her vinyl apron. Geez, what was it with him? With *her*? She'd never objectified a man before. She pressed her lips together. She should be ashamed of herself.

'A foster carer's housekeeper. As a kid I was fascinated by chemical reactions. On a TV programme I discovered the pantry was filled with exciting opportunities, so after a spectacular volcano with some baking soda and vinegar that spread considerably further than I'd imagined, rather than risk me blowing up the place, Mrs Tracey put me to work. She gave me a love for cooking.' A fleeting smile touched his lips.

Olivia grinned, imagining the young Jett. 'Sounds like you two had lots of fun.'

The animation in his expression dropped away and his hand tightened briefly on the whisk. 'I was shifted elsewhere a few months later.'

'Why?' The word popped out in spite of telling herself she wasn't going to ask.

He shook his head, dipped a finger into the mix and touched it to her mouth. 'Why, indeed.' Dark eyes met hers. Challenging her. 'Taste.'

When she went totally still, he rubbed his finger sensuously along her lower lip. 'Come on, taste.'

Oh...my. Seduction by muffin mix. She closed her lips over his finger. The batter swirled sweetly over her tongue; a hint of masculine soap drifted to her nose. She swayed a bit to the rolling movement of the yacht beneath her feet as she sucked him in deeper and scraped her teeth over his finger. Watched the surprise in his gaze turn to red-hot desire. She drew back instantly, super-aware of their own highly volatile chemical reaction in progress.

Who had seduced whom? Even semi-incapacitated he lured her. His willingness—or was it sheer stubbornness?— to ignore his discomfort for the crew's sake. Wiping the back of her hand across her tingling lips, she stepped away. 'Leave you to it. I'll be on deck if you n... I'll be on deck.'

She heard him chuckle as she fled.

Late in the afternoon of the third day they were within hours of crossing the finish line. Olivia watched Tasmania's rugged coastline through misty eyes and her heart ached. *I know you're here somewhere, Mum. Sharing the dream we made together. And I've been good. Had the test as you requested.*

'Are you okay?' Brie murmured beside her.

Olivia startled. She was aware her eyes were stinging. 'I didn't hear you come up.' She sniffed, searched for that elusive tissue in her pocket, then blew her nose. 'Sea air,' she mumbled.

She knew Brie wasn't fooled. They both stared at the coast. 'Your mum would be proud.'

Olivia lifted her shoulders, hugged her arms, her eyes fixed dead ahead.

'*I'm* proud,' Brie continued. 'Not just of the race. I'm proud of you. Taking that test took guts.' Olivia felt her friend's gaze. 'And I'll be here for you whatever happens, you know that.'

Olivia rubbed at the ache in her chest, still watching the horizon. 'I know. I'll be back in a jiffy.'

'Take your time,' Brie told her. 'Everything's fine and you're dead on your feet. I'll let you know when to come up.'

'I won't be long.' Olivia made her way below deck and stretched out on the other berth for just a minute, the one blessedly free from any trace of masculine scents or clothing or reminders.

She'd hardly slept for the entire voyage, responsibility on her shoulders, and aware every moment that she was making this trip without the person who'd meant so much to her. 'Mum,' she whispered. 'You'd be impressed with what we've achieved.' Having Jett aboard had been an unexpected bonus, giving their Snowflake savings account a real boost.

But had her rash challenge to Jett been about the foundation? Or was it more about having him see her as strong and competent? To keep him around because she wanted to see more of him before he took off? And wasn't there also that sneaky itch to get back at him for mocking a female's expertise in a traditionally male-dominated role?

Yet he'd used his own expertise yesterday—in a traditionally female-dominated role—cooking up delicious treats for them when she'd known he was still under the weather. He'd kept a sense of humour about it all when he could have spent his free time sleeping it off.

The crew had loved it. They loved *him*—naturally. She'd never seen them go to such lengths to please and she was *not* jealous of the respect and attention he gave back to each crew member. Okay, she was. A little. But most of all, she admired his good-humoured participation. He'd gone above and beyond what she'd expected from a playboy chef suffering seasickness. He'd kept to his word and not distracted her during the trip—at least not intentionally.

Then last night when she'd come to switch watches, he'd stopped awhile to talk about her future fundraising plans. What she hoped to achieve. As if he was *interested*.

Then as he left, he'd mentioned their 'unfinished business'. Caught off guard, she'd told him again that the only important thing to her was the race and Snowflake. That she wasn't interested in anything more than his friendship.

He'd taken her at her word and disappeared down the hatch too damn quickly for her self-esteem.

A mistake, she'd decided. A no-strings fling with a gorgeous, intelligent and attentive guy was exactly what she needed right now.

Need.

A word she hated.

She rolled onto her back and stared at the overhead a few inches from her nose. She was *not* one of those needy women who required a man in their lives to make them feel complete. She was doing fine on her own, thanks very much. But distraction; she could have done with some of that… Her eyes drifted closed, the yacht's gentle motion carrying her away.

When she next opened her eyes, the flicker from a low-hung lantern cast a glow over the dim, wood-panelled cabin. She'd slept longer than she'd meant to. The air smelled oddly of old spices over the rich aroma of stewed meat.

'You're awake, my pretty.'

At the low growl of appreciation accompanying the words, she turned her head on the pillow and what she saw took her breath away. He was magnificent. Gloriously naked from the waist up, dark breeches riding low on lean hips, held there by a length of rope. The edge of a cutlass glinted beside one muscled thigh.

'Jett?'

He grinned. A sailor's grin. A sinner's grin. A grin that turned her inner thighs to jelly and made her woman's flesh burn.

Lamp glow gilded his swarthy skin, purple shadows carving deep valleys over the rugged terrain of his chest and shadowing the granite cliff of a jaw. As if viewing someone else, Olivia glanced down at herself, realising she wore a gauzy white gown as sheer as it was simple…and where was her underwear?

Her arms were crossed at the wrists, bound with silky cords and placed above her head on the pillow so that her breasts pouted up at him like an offering. Her legs sprawled across the bed, her ankles bound with the same silky cord and tied to the bedposts.

'Captain Jett Black at your service.' His reply was whisky-smooth arrogance and rich with innuendo. And didn't that name suit his looks and soul perfectly?

Those *jet-black* eyes traced an impertinent path over her face to her rapidly tightening nipples, her belly...lower, sensuous coils of heat drifting over her skin.

She writhed on the bed, rough sheets chafing ultrasensitised flesh. 'But you're a pirate.'

'I'm your fantasy.'

'No!'

But her breathing quickened as he slid a callused hand between her trembling thighs and inched the hem of her gown up over her knees. Higher...

'I don't need a man in my life.'

'I'm here to prove you wrong. You'll surrender to me. What's more you'll do it willingly.'

Her head thrashed on the pillow. 'I'll never surrender.'

He bent his head and sucked a nipple through the sheer fabric, the moist decadent heat of his mouth making her arch her back and cry out.

She couldn't think. Not with his fingers sliding along her moist flesh, then plunging deep, drawing out slowly only to push inside once more, over and over, dazzling her with unspeakable delights, unimaginable pleasure.

'You want me,' he whispered, his breath harsh against her ear, his palm hot and hard and heaven as he ruched the fabric up over her concave belly, the dip of her waist, leaving her exposed to his lusty gaze. Vulnerable and on the edge of insanity.

'No...'

He shifted lower, his perfectly sculpted masculine body sliding over hers. Down. His stubble chafed on delicate skin, then soothed the sudden tenderness with lazy laps of his tongue. On the brink and helpless, she looked down her body and met his eyes and knew what he was going to do. He grinned then bent his head.

'Yes,' she moaned, throwing her head back and giving herself up to the glory. Surrendering gladly. 'Yes!'

'You're as needy as all the rest.' He slid off the end of the bed and stood, a triumphant smirk on his pirate lips. 'Maybe more.'

She blinked awake to find Jett watching her, a mug of something steaming in his hands. 'Just as I thought.'

She cringed beneath his scrutiny, her lower body throbbing with unsatisfied desire. *'What?'*

'I said you needed the rest.'

Her hands rushed to pull the light blanket she'd thrown over herself earlier up to her chin. 'No, I meant what are you *doing here*?' She prayed she hadn't moaned or called out or worse.

'Waiting for you to wake up.' He raised the mug. 'Thought you might need a cup of green tea. You've hardly slept a wink the entire trip.'

'I don't *need anything* from you.' She struggled to sit up, still holding the blanket close and glaring at him, hoping he'd take the hint and disappear. How could she have dreamed of *him* when it was her mother she'd come in here to be close to? To think about? And she'd hardly thought of her mum at all. Guilty heat rose up her neck.

'A grumpy riser.' His shoulders lifted and bunched, his thumbs rubbing the side of the mug. 'A sure sign you didn't get enough. Sleep,' he clarified, a hint of humour in his eyes.

'Don't you have something to do? A watch to be on?' A plank to walk?

'Free as a bird. Which reminds me, you missed the albatross we spotted off the starboard side about thirty minutes ago.'

'Thirty minutes ago?' She swung her legs over the side of the bunk.

'That's a sign of good luck, right?'

'I hope so.' A thought struck her as her feet hit the floor with a thud. 'Isn't your surname Davies?'

'It was my mother's name. Why?'

'Never mind. Thanks for the tea.' She indicated a cubby-hole beside the bunk preferring to avoid even the slightest possibility of skin contact lest she spontaneously combust in an inferno of lust. 'Here's fine.' *Now go away.*

He set it down. 'Brie says to tell you we'll have a fair wind the rest of the way and all is under control.'

'Tell Brie I'll be five minutes.'

The instant he'd gone, she blew out the breath she'd been holding and hugged her knees to her chest. She wished *she* were under control. Ever since she'd met this man her hold on life as she knew it seemed to be slipping away.

'Skipper?'

She whipped her head around to see him there again.

'Just so you know, I won't be participating in any after-race celebrations.'

'That's up to you. You've done more than enough for our cause, so thank you.' She picked up her tea, lifted it to her lips and studied him over the rim, telling herself she wasn't disappointed. 'Sick of our company already, huh?'

'I've got other plans.'

'But you and Brie—'

'Already arranged.'

'Oh. Great. Good.'

He started to turn then stopped, raised a finger as if something had slipped his mind. 'Another thing. I won't be pursuing our promised discussion. If you were expecting me to call,' he added.

'Fine.' She said it like an accusation. Her fingers tightened on the mug. 'Why not?' The fragile words spilled free before she could censor them, which only infuriated her further. She'd been so determined not to come across as that *needy* woman.

'You made it clear that's the way you want it. I respect that.' But he reached out, tucked a loose strand of her hair behind her ear and she caught a whiff of his soap on his hands. 'Breanna has my phone number if you change your mind.'

She watched him turn and leave. He'd done some thinking on board and decided Olivia's type didn't appeal to his sophisticated taste. Probably relieved she'd knocked his offer back.

A part of her wished he hadn't, another part earned her respect.

CHAPTER EIGHT

'Jett's gone into lockdown because he doesn't want any more media hassles,' Brie told Olivia as she packed her bag. She was flying to one of tropical northern Queensland's remote islands with some fellow beauty therapists later this afternoon. 'I think he's well and truly done his bit. Which means he could probably do with some company. Being on his own and all.'

Olivia and Brie had been staying in one of Hobart's luxury hotels near the waterfront, recuperating after the race and enjoying Tassie's Taste Festival. Despite their upgraded suite having three master bedrooms, Jett had conveniently found accommodation in the penthouse upstairs. Who else but the Jettsetter Chef would be able to source five-star penthouse accommodation in a fully booked city during the busiest week on Hobart's calendar?

The press had swooped and swarmed all over him when they'd docked. Olivia had been surprised and eternally grateful for his good humour towards the reporters—he'd been a genuine and enthusiastic spokesperson for the foundation, even agreeing to an appearance on the local TV morning show in the coming week.

So Brie had told her.

Because Olivia hadn't seen or heard from him since he'd walked away from *Chasing Dawn* at the marina.

'Liv, did you hear me?'

'Yes.' Olivia looked up from the novel she was trying to read. 'Company.' She'd never liked the taste of sour grapes but there was a whole bunch in her mouth right now. She knew Brie and Jett had caught up. She hadn't asked for details but he was obviously the reason for Brie's happy demeanour. 'What sort of *company* are we talking about?'

'Companionship. For starters anyway. You can move on for the main course if things go well.' Brie tossed a new orange bikini on top of her overstuffed bag. 'It's New Year's Eve tomorrow. And I know for a fact his evening's free. Like yours.'

'What if I've made plans and I just haven't told you?'

Brie looked her over, brows raised. 'Have you?'

Olivia ran a lazy finger over her e-reader's screen, waited for the next page to load. 'Maybe.' She continued staring at her reader.

'I know you, my friend, and there's not a chance. He's leaving on New Year's Day,' Brie continued. 'To work on his new book.'

'Inspirational spot, Cradle Mountain. I'm sure he'll enjoy it.'

Brie let out a long-suffering sigh and walked over to where Olivia was curled up on the couch and stuck her hands on her hips. 'It's New Year and you have the hots for each other.'

Olivia glanced up. 'So? Are you saying I should phone him up and ask for sex?'

Brie's grin was fast and wide. 'As long as you're careful. He's a casual sort of guy and I know you're not...'

'Experienced.' Olivia stretched lazily, waggled her fingers. 'Maybe it *is* time I tried something different. And if I want to play with fire I've got to expect to get a little singed along the way, right?' She dropped her hands and picked up her reader again. 'Having said that, nothing's going to happen.'

'Hey, I've seen you two look at each other and it's combustion central. So I'm saying yes, definitely try that new adventure, have some fun—you both deserve it.'

Combustion central? Not any more. She'd told him no. He'd accepted it. 'We admitted the attraction. Now we've moved on.'

'Yeah, right.' Brie patted Olivia's hand then rose and walked to her wheely bag. 'It's not too late to ask him down for a drink,' she said as she checked her purse. 'Or if you're feeling shy, you could meet in the lobby, go somewhere on the waterfront and enjoy the view. Oh, and for your convenience, I've put his phone number in your contacts list.'

'Me? Ask him?' Olivia's chin lifted. 'And I'm not shy.'

'I know you're not—usually. You're an equal rights ambassador and you demonstrated that to him very clearly, more than once.' She cocked her head to one side. 'Maybe he feels threatened.'

'Threatened? Jett?' Olivia laughed—a little hysterically—and stood too, hands in the pockets of her jeans as she walked to the door to see Brie off. 'Is this the same guy we're talking about?'

'He's my brother, obviously I don't see him the same way you do. Happy New Year,' Brie said against her cheek. 'Go out and have a good time.'

'Yep.'

Brie studied her a moment. 'You're really not even going to try, are you? I should have insisted you come with us instead of letting you opt out as you always do.' She pulled out her phone to check her messages, then opened the door. 'Phone coverage isn't reliable that far north. If anything urgent happens...'

'Nothing's going to happen. I'm going to open a bottle of

champagne and drink it in the spa then go downstairs and enjoy the street party. Have a great trip.'

New Year's Eve on Hobart's city streets was alive with people and action. Eyes disguised behind a pair of reflective sunglasses, Jett stepped out of the crowded hotel lobby and into a cab. Knowing trouble was in the same hotel alone and a few floors below him, he needed the distraction. He watched the casino's twinkling lights come into view.

Endless opportunities abounded in love and luck with plenty of attractive women on the prowl. If he chose, he could celebrate the stroke of midnight back in his room with a bottle of chilled champagne, and a willing body to slake another kind of thirst.

To his surprise and chagrin, the thought of spending the evening going at it with a faceless woman he'd never see again left him cold. Ten minutes after setting out, he was back in the hotel, scowling. What the hell? He was never indecisive.

If he wanted to rid himself of a case of inconvenient lust for a leggy redhead, there had to be another option.

A swim in the pool? A cold shower? Only one thing was going to rid him of the simmering heat in his veins—and it wasn't happening: she'd made it abundantly clear it wasn't happening. He watched revellers spilling out of the popular restaurants around Sullivan's Cove and knocked back a can of soda.

The muted TV screen was showing ten minutes to midnight. Swapping his handmade silk shirt for a soft worn jersey, he poured himself a large Scotch from the suite's minibar, drank it down. He was looking forward to a few hours of oblivion.

Olivia pressed her lips together and waited for Jett to answer the intercom to his penthouse apartment. She was wearing a stupid party hat and juggling a supermarket bag filled with New Year cheer and her nerves were stretched to breaking point.

Three hours ago she'd been eating a late dinner alone in the hotel room, listening to other people having fun, watching the celebrations from her balcony. Where would she be next New Year? Next New Year, she'd know—one way or another. She'd wanted to reach out, grab hold of life with both hands while she still could and join in.

Her focus had been so narrow, so sharply defined by the goals she'd set for herself. The race, the fundraising and memories of her mother had reminded her that time was a gift that couldn't be bought or bartered for and could be snatched away without warning.

And she'd made a decision. Changed her mind. Jett. Tonight. This was her chance to take time for herself before she knew for sure what her future held. The result would surely be positive. She'd have no choice then but to make those difficult decisions she'd put at the back of her mind for so long. Surgery. Lifestyle.

But not tonight. Not even next week.

She'd had the entrée with Jett, and Brie was right—she wanted the main course.

She shifted impatiently on the balls of her feet. What if he wasn't in? What if he was sharing a New Year's bonk with some other random woman he'd picked up? The way he'd done with *her* on Christmas Eve?

She heard a crackle through the speaker then, 'Olivia.' The disembodied voice didn't sound particularly pleased.

He had the advantage and she wished the video worked both ways so she could see his expression. So she'd know whether she was making an idiot of herself. She tapped her silly hat and smiled. 'You still recognise me, then.'

The pause lasted long enough to write Happy New Year with a blocked glitter pen. 'What's up?'

'Brie mentioned you were on your own tonight… And since I…' She trailed off, biting back the needy, desperate words on the tip of her tongue.

Dammit, she wasn't taking no for an answer. She wasn't *needy*—she was taking control. She rose up on tiptoes, closer to the intercom as if to draw him into her game. 'It's nine minutes to midnight. Let me in, I want to wish you Happy New Year.' She glanced at the bag in her arms. 'And I've got stuff.'

'Stuff.'

'Eight minutes thirty seconds and counting.'

The elevator doors to his penthouse slid open to her left.

Relieved, with dignity intact—for now at least—she stepped inside. And was tempted to back out again. The mirror on the back wall reflected a woman with wild red hair topped with a green foil cone hat on an odd tilt, eyes too wide for her face. Freckles and fine lines from years of sailing in the sun. Definitely not Jett's type—oh yeah, she'd looked him up on the Internet and seen his type.

She'd only hooked his attention the first time because it had been dim and she'd looked half decent in her new fire-engine-red cocktail dress. Tonight she was wearing an avocado-coloured ankle-length shift and gold sandals. Nothing too sexy and provocative in case he'd changed his mind about spending the night alone and had another woman up here.

Her fingers clenched around the bag. She'd die of embarrassment, she'd just die— 'Hi,' she said, breezing out as the door opened, *not* looking at him and heading straight for the fantastic view taking up one whole wall. The only light in the room came from outside and the muted TV screen.

'Wow, look at that. The penthouse view. Almost as pretty as Sydney Harbour.'

'You're a Taswegian, you're biased.' His voice, a mellow baritone, stroked up her spine and her eyes slid closed. His woodsy soap she'd become familiar with during the race teased her nostrils. His presence behind her filled her with a new kind of longing.

Turning, she set her bag of goodies on the smoked-glass dining table where his computer blinked and now she *did* look at the reason she was here.

Rumpled and casual in shorts that might have been white once upon a time and a soft-looking black T-shirt. The tight fit outlined hard-packed muscles and those powerful legs, which had caught her attention that first night, were tantalisingly bare from mid-thigh down. 'You're an Apple Islander too.'

With only a dim light in the corner, the dusky air was thick with tension. He furrowed a hand through tousled hair, obviously not for the first time tonight. 'I think you should go.'

She smiled and reached for her bag while butterflies swarmed in her belly. Stepped out of her sandals. 'That's silly, I just got here.'

Reaching into her bag, she placed the contents on the table one at a time. A bottle of her favourite sparkling white, a punnet of strawberries, a supermarket's pre-packed selection of cheeses. Grapes.

His reaction might have been bored, as if he was used to women bearing gifts, except for a telltale twitch at the corner of his mouth before he said, 'What's all this?'

'It's New Year…' she glanced at the countdown on the silent TV '…in four minutes and twenty seconds. And I want to celebrate.' Digging deeper, she snatched up one of those party favours that unrolled like a tongue and made a funny noise, and blew it at him.

No response.

'Party popper, then?' She snatched it from her bag of surprises and pulled. It sounded like a gunshot in the silence. 'Oh, for goodness' sakes.' Exasperated, she tossed the explosion of tiny streamers at him and moved to the TV, raised the volume so she could hear the party happening in front of the Opera House and Harbour Bridge. 'So...it's me.' She waited on tenterhooks, breath backing up in her throat.

'Yeah. And you're still trouble,' he said, finally, and maybe she saw a glint of humour in his eye before it vanished as quick as a blink.

She let out a relieved breath. 'Good. That's good. I think. Okay. It's New Year.'

'So it is.'

Slapping sweat-damp hands on her thighs, she glanced once at the screen where revellers were having fun at Circular Quay. 'Three minutes.' Nodding at the foil hat, she set to work uncorking the bottle of bubbly. 'I don't want to be the only one looking ridiculous.'

He shook his head. 'Ridiculous, never. You look gorgeous. Sexy and gorgeous and damn near irresistible.'

Her blood turned to syrup but she kept her tone light. 'Why thank you. Glasses?' As she ripped the foil she watched him walk to the bar and collect two tumblers rather than the crystal flutes. Fine. She wasn't going to quibble about details.

The cork popped and a cheery fizzing sound filled the room. 'Tassie's best.' She filled the glasses while he held them out, then set the bottle on the table. Their fingers barely touched as he handed her a glass but it was enough to send a *whoosh* through her skittering pulse. It hadn't done that since the last time Jett had touched her. She looked up into dark, unreadable eyes. 'Happy New Year, Jett Davies.'

'And you.'

They took a mouthful and she let the bubbles slide down her throat then licked the sweetness from her lips and said, 'If you won't, I will.' Grabbing the little foil cap, she reached up and set it on top of his head, secured the elastic beneath his chin with a little *ping* and a grin. 'Forty-five seconds till lip-lock time.' Her gaze dropped to his mouth and temptation ruled. 'Or we could start early.'

She didn't know who moved first but she was aware of two things: his lips were on hers…and she wasn't counting down those last seconds to midnight.

All she could do was focus on the guy she was kissing. Tasting of champagne and musky man and sweet, sweet temptation. Making her head spin. Driving her crazy and sending her to that place he'd shown her. That place she couldn't wait to revisit.

The instant their mouths touched, Jett couldn't resist. She was spontaneous and fun and her lips soft and warm and generous. Without thought he banded his arms around her and pulled her close, her body pliant and melting against his like brandy custard over plum pudding.

He heard the television's countdown click over to the New Year and lifted his head to look at the enchanting vision in front of him. The exploding fireworks outside showered colour over her face.

Stars shone in her eyes and her lips curved as she met his gaze. 'Happy New Year,' she said, softly. 'Again.'

He couldn't help but smile back as he let his hands roam lower, to the firm curve of her backside, and tucked her tighter to him, grinding his pelvis hard against her. 'Back at you.'

She groaned at the contact, her sweet breath fanning his

face. 'It's pretty good so far.' Grin widening, she cupped her hands around his jaw and pulled his face back to hers. He was more than happy to oblige, enjoying the way her fingers moved into his hair, against his scalp. Firm and flexible. Sure and strong. Competent. He closed his eyes and tried *not* to imagine how they'd feel manipulating other parts of his tight, tortured body.

He ran his hands lightly up her spine and she gave one of those little shivers of delight and leaned closer. Firm breasts pressed against his chest, hard nipples easily felt through the thin layers of fabric separating them. She was aroused. Ready. And so, so tempting.

Except Olivia wasn't the kind of good-time girl he enjoyed briefly before moving on. No matter how enthusiastic Olivia was to get on with it, no matter how willing he was to let her. She was also Breanna's best friend—definitely not to be messed with.

So this kiss was absolutely a one-off. A souvenir. Just for fun, for New Year.

Except it felt like…more.

Her unique flavour was as exotic as any taste sensation he could concoct, drawing him into some kind of maelstrom that made his head spin and his heart pound in a crazy way.

He told himself it was the Scotch he'd drunk, that he'd not eaten since breakfast, that he was still recovering from seasickness, but, like an addict, he couldn't seem to tear his lips away.

He wasn't aware how long they stood there locked together from neck to knees and mouth to mouth but finally they both had to come up for air.

It was the break he needed to pull himself out of the spell he seemed to be under. His breathing was unsteady and he struggled for cool, clear sanity. Cursing silently, he ripped off the party hat, tossed it to the floor. Gripping her upper arms, he looked into her eyes, determined to ignore the tempting invitation he saw there. 'This is not a good idea.' He spoke each word slowly and deliberately as much for himself as for her.

Olivia watched him through a fog of desire swamped with frustration. Because she knew it was mutual—his dark gaze and the hard, hot ridge of masculine flesh between them proved his words were a lie. She tossed her own hat away. 'Why?'

'Because if you stay, we're going to finish what we started a week ago. You're killing me here, skipper.'

Her spine tingled with the thrill that his admission brought. She wasn't going anywhere. She pushed at his chest. 'I changed my mind about being with you. And don't look so worried, it's just for fun. I know that.'

'Fun,' he echoed, his brows drawing together as if he didn't think her capable of such a notion.

'You're not a one-woman guy—you don't even trust people enough to make friends—so yes, fun. What else would it be?' Olivia picked up the supermarket bag still within reach on the table. Her hand trembled a bit as she drew out a smaller paper bag from the bottom.

His eyes darted to her package, back to hers. Heat smouldered in their depths, scarlet smudges flared high on his cheekbones. 'What trouble are you planning on getting us into now?'

'*I've* decided we need to finish whatever this is between us before we move on. And we're going to finish it.' She waved the paper bag in front of his face, opened it carefully. 'That's why I brought condoms.'

'Olivia…'

Letting the bag fall to the floor, she held up the packets. 'I didn't know what you prefer so I got three. Ridged, ultra lubricated and extra l—'

'Stop.' Placing a thumb against her mouth, he sealed off the rest of her sentence. 'Just stop.'

But Olivia refused to stop. She wanted him, and she was going to have him. She pried his thumb from her mouth and told him, 'We're just getting started.'

CHAPTER NINE

SHE'D NEVER PLAYED a seductress-in-the-bedroom game. Never wanted to, never even been tempted and certainly wasn't sure she knew how. But something deeper urged Olivia to try. *Tomorrow might be too late.*

And with Jett, it would be too late because this was their last night in Hobart. Tomorrow they'd go their separate ways. If they met up again—through Brie—it might be under very different personal circumstances.

She tucked the condom packets in the pocket of his shorts, then, since her hands were already in the vicinity, she took the opportunity to slide her fingers under his T-shirt. And up. She felt the hard muscles beneath his skin contract beneath her touch.

A strangled sound issued from his throat. She liked the sense of power his reaction gave her. That she could turn him on. She could get him to play.

'Your skin's so hot,' she murmured, rubbing her hands over two flat male nipples as she gained confidence, stepping into the role with apparent ease. 'Maybe you'd feel cooler if we just…take this…off.' Heart pounding, she waited, her eyes on his, and saw a battle waging within their dark depths.

'You'd better be sure about this,' he said. 'Because tomorrow I'm gone.'

'I know. And I'm sure.' Once started, her newly discovered inner seductress made it so easy to slip her hands onto his bare shoulders, lean in and convince him with her mouth, with her tongue. With a slide of her bare foot over his shin and up, agile toes finding purchase on the back of a hairy thigh.

He reared back, muttering something unintelligible, but his hands shot upwards and the T-shirt was gone, leaving a bronzed expanse of skin sprinkled with dark hair that arrowed down and disappeared beneath the waistband of his shorts.

Olivia dared her gaze to follow. Her mouth went dry, her legs turned to jelly and her core throbbed with desire and anticipation. He was even bigger than she remembered. Oh. Sweet. Heaven. Would all that fit? She couldn't wait to find out.

He reached for the straps of her dress but she shook him off. 'My turn tonight.'

He nodded, eyes heavy and smoking hot in the dimness. 'Help yourself.'

He appeared all casualness and acquiescence but Olivia could see the tension rippling across his abdomen. Perhaps he enjoyed having women perform sexual favours for him, or he was humouring her for the moment, because no way would he play the passive role unless it suited him. Even now, she knew he could turn this situation around and have her pinned beneath him before she could blink.

That made him dangerous. And exciting.

She reached out and touched him, a light stroke across his abdomen, a fingertip against his navel. 'Are you a brief or boxer man?' She slid both hands beneath his waistband. Her knuckles grazed firm, warm skin.

'Guess you're about to find out for yourself.' His voice sounded low, strained.

'Not here.' She prodded him so that he walked backwards

until his calves came up against a wide leather recliner chair, then nodded. 'Here's good.'

She reached into his pocket for condoms—she wasn't fussed which packet it was—and slapped them on the coffee table beside the chair. Then with a nerve she hadn't known she possessed until this minute, she shoved the shorts—and boxers too—over his hips and down. There was an awkward moment when he had to help her manipulate the fabric over his massive erection, but then he was stepping out of them and kicking them aside and he was naked and she was fully clothed and she felt amazing and powerful and sexy.

He cleared his throat. 'Do you want me to lie down?'

'Not yet.' Outside, the party lived on but the only sound in the room was their quickened breathing and her heart beating its way out of her chest. She shifted closer, felt his need, warm and tempting across the intimate space between them. Like a kid with a new discovery, she was compelled to touch, to explore. She'd never touched a man this way and curiosity and wonder filled her. Hot, silk-covered steel. Wrapping her hands around him, she looked up, watched his eyes darken as she acquainted herself with him. She experimented, squeezing gently and sliding her hand upwards. 'Wow.'

He shuddered, placed a firm grip on her shoulders. 'You keep doing that and it's going to be over in seconds.' His voice was gruff, his jaw tight.

She bit her bottom lip, and immediately let go. 'Sorry...'

A glimmer of what looked like humour lit his eyes. 'You're kidding, right?'

'I...it's just that you make me want to be adventurous and a little bit naughty.'

He grinned. 'Hell, skipper, you're already adventurous. And I'm all for a little bit of naughty.' He pulled her against him and toppled them both onto the butter-soft leather.

'Hey, it was my turn.' But she laughed, breathless, and

straddled him, arms straight, hands resting on his broad shoulders. His legs chafed against her inner thighs, his arousal nestled huge and hot against her panties.

He waggled his brows at her. 'You're on top, aren't you?'

She looked down at the seemingly innocuous smile with wicked fun smouldering in those dark eyes. 'Yeah...'

It was the oddest feeling being with this man with a playboy reputation—the sort of man she usually had little time for. But she knew now that it was only a part of who he was, and right now he just made her feel special.

He tugged the zip at the back of her dress, his fingers grazing a shivery path down her spine along the way. It slid from her shoulders to hang, gaping and loose on his chest. His eyes didn't leave hers, glittering in the dimness as he flicked open her bra, pulling it away from her skin and exposing her tightening nipples to the cool air.

'You're amazing, you know that?' he told her while big palms smoothed the fabric up over her outer thighs, raising goose-bumps and heat and blood pressure.

She shifted, adjusting her knees so she was closer. 'This whole night's amazing.'

Jett agreed, his hands sweeping up the curves of her body as he divested her of her clothing. Then she was exposed to his gaze but for a pair of skimpy lace knickers and he took a moment to go slow, trailing his fingers over peaches and cream skin never touched by the sun. Pert pink nipples ripe for tasting. He filled his hands with her sensational breasts and listened to her breathing quicken and turn choppy, then raised his head and suckled her.

'Jett...'

Gasping, she threw back her head and Jett felt her nails digging crescent moons deep into his shoulders. He tipped back his head to see her better. Her lips were pressed together, her eyes closed.

'Right here with you,' he murmured.

She made a little sound at the back of her throat.

Ah...yeah. He wanted to hear those cute little noises she made when she came. He wanted to hear them *now*.

But more than that, he wanted *her*. Only her. All of her. He admired her control-freak nature, he'd found it a turn-on and he'd never want to break it, but tonight he wanted to bend that control. Just a little. To watch her fly apart and know he was responsible. He reached down between their bodies and with two swift tugs the last lacy barrier disappeared.

Her eyes went round with surprise, but only for a moment before her mouth kicked up at the corners. 'That was my best pair of knickers. I wore them especially for you.'

'And I appreciated them, believe me.' Without taking his gaze off her, he grabbed the condom packet, tore one open and sheathed himself. Something flickered at the edge of his consciousness, like sheet lightning on the ocean's horizon on a sultry summer night. Olivia wasn't like other women he slept with. And tomorrow— Nuh. He reached for her. She was here now, she wanted him, and for tonight she was his.

As his hands gripped her waist and lifted her hips she drew in a sharp breath and Olivia saw doubt cross his gaze. Still gripping his shoulders to support herself on arms that had started to tremble, she met his eyes. 'It's okay.'

He slowed, setting her down carefully on his belly. 'Please tell me you've done this before.'

Heat rushed to her cheeks. 'I have. But not often.' She bit her lips then said, 'I'm sorry.'

Dark eyes searched hers, brows lowered. 'What are you apologising for this time?'

'Because...I'm not very good.' Her most intimate parts on full view, she'd never felt more exposed. Except he wasn't looking at her intimate parts; his gaze was focused on her eyes.

'Who the hell told you that?'

'Jason… An ex-boyfriend. He said…'

'He was an idiot and he was wrong. And you're not getting away from me that easily.'

'Really?' Relief washed through her.

'Really.' A corner of his mouth lifted and he touched her cheek. 'We'll take it slow.' With an infinitely tender gaze, one she'd never thought Jett capable of, he drew her head down until their lips touched, ever so lightly. A butterfly's kiss that soothed and enticed.

And for a rare and precious moment she felt like that emerging butterfly—shiny and new, treasured even. She felt as if he were kissing her for the first time, his lips surprisingly gentle and so, so sweet, fingers tangling lightly in her hair and drawing it down so the tips caressed his shoulders. Creating a curtain so that all she could see when she lifted her lips and opened her eyes was the perfection of his face.

'Everything okay?' he murmured.

'I just want to look at you.' He stared at her and again she sensed his hesitation. 'Don't freak out,' she said tight-lipped. 'I have no interest in long term either, if that's what you're wondering.'

'Here isn't the right place for this.' Somehow he managed to push up, tucking her against him. She clung to his neck as he carried her across the entertainment area, down a short passage and into a luxury bedroom.

She got a glimpse of a massive bed piled with cushions and strewn with discarded clothes but then he tumbled her onto a cool cotton quilt and followed her down.

Stark white street lights shone through shuttered windows throwing silver bars across the bed as he stretched out, pulling her on top of him again, but slowly and close so that every exquisitely sensitive part of her slid along every hard and hot and masculine part of him.

Jett kept his hands casual and easy, his movements slow

and loose, but heat glimmered beneath skin, a banked fire—one spark and they'd both ignite. 'Just so you know, I want you too,' he murmured.

A purely female smile tugged at her lips. 'It's kind of obvious.' She straddled him again, one hand in the centre of his chest as she wriggled downwards. 'And while I'm on top I'm going to take full advantage.'

'I meant...' That swift silvery tug had snagged him mid-sternum. Caught him unawares. 'You're one of a kind.'

Her apricot fragrance surrounded him with warmth—and something more. It took a heartbeat or two to recognise it. Familiarity. And intimacy that went beyond the physical. He was unaccustomed to both. Solitary was his life. No hassles, no heartaches.

He'd be on the road out of town first thing tomorrow.

For now he concentrated on guiding himself to her entrance and arousing her with slow smooth strokes while she supported herself on her arms in such a way so that her breasts grazed his chest. The inexperienced seducing the player with the kind of sweet torture he almost wished could last for ever.

'We won't do anything until you're ready.'

Her laughter, surprisingly earthy, filled the quiet room. 'My one and only Secret Sinner-Santa. I've been ready for you since Christmas Eve.'

Unlike her robust amusement, beneath the cold white light filtering through the shutters her usually sun-kissed skin took on the fragile appearance of delicate porcelain, and he discovered *he* was the one trembling. Apparently his sexy skipper was as daring in the bedroom as she was on the ocean.

Fascinating, Olivia thought, how a man's body could be so different but fit so beautifully with hers. He'd set the mood to mellow, the pace to slow and for now she was happy to go with it.

Slow didn't mean less intense, oh no. For her tonight, the journey was as important as the destination. And since this was a one-off, she intended to make it last. All the way to Morningtown.

'Olivia…'

She'd noticed Jett only used her real name when something was serious. She looked down, met his eyes and saw something tender, almost vulnerable, beneath the raw and primitive. When she blinked it was gone.

'Jett…' she murmured back, instinctively lowering her mouth to his to soothe and assuage and distract. And seduce.

He gripped her jaw and let his lips slide over hers, back and forth. 'I'm glad you changed your mind.'

She nibbled the shell of his ear and whispered, 'So am I.'

'I love your breasts,' he murmured, his lips and tongue teasing the ruched tips.

Her breath caught. One day those breasts he so admired would betray her. She wondered vaguely how he'd feel about her if they were gone. How any man would feel about a woman who was only half a woman.

'Anything wrong?' He paused and his gaze flicked to hers, concerns and questions in their depths.

'Nothing,' she whispered, pushing bad thoughts away, pulling his head down to her breast again. 'Don't stop.' Her fingers tightened as she stroked his silky hair. 'Give me everything. *I want it all.*'

No lover could have been more caring and attentive and patient than Jett. The low rumble of his voice, the unhurried way he moved his hands over her. He knew just where to touch, to taste, how to make her body sing with nothing more than words.

Lovely lingering caresses, slow murmurs, exquisitely sensual. The drift of light over his face. Nerves melting away in the warmth of his gaze. Time to savour, to enjoy.

There was nothing but this moment, this place. This man. Her mind was filled with him, lazy limbs sliding against his, the scent of their mingled bodies rising up between them.

His muscles were taut, humming, and she knew what it was costing a hot-blooded, experienced man like Jett to go so slowly. A considerate lover, allowing her to set the pace, to take control.

There were no words exchanged as they explored one another. Just murmurs of delight at each new discovery. The way he shuddered when she licked inside his ear. The feel of corded muscle beneath firm skin. Contrasts and textures. She'd never thought a man's body would be so appealing to touch or feel so pleasurable against hers.

And when the unrelenting passion drove her to the point of madness, she lowered her body onto his heat and strength and, with a sigh of delight, she took him inside her. Their gazes fused and pleasure reigned. She arched and slowly began to move with him.

Finally, this time when she reached that glorious vortex, he was right there with her, sharing the flash and sizzle as they took flight over the edge together.

Neither of them moved for several minutes. Or it might have been hours. She might have slept but she was sure she hadn't. How could she sleep after the most amazing experience of her life? All she was sure of was that this guy lying beside her, his breathing slow and even and a hairy thigh resting heavy between her legs, was out for the count.

No pillow talk, then. And it wasn't what she and Jett were about anyway. One night was all it had ever been, all it would ever be; they both understood that. And she was relieved he was asleep because it would make it easier to slip away, redress and let herself out—*sans* panties.

No need for conversation. No awkward moments and face-to-face morning-after. She needed time alone to think about the night, to replay it in her mind—and store it in her heart.

Because in spite of all the warnings she'd given herself, she was falling for him. Falling for him in a bigger way than she'd ever dreamed of. Oh, he was a playboy and way too sure of himself, but the more time she spent with him, the more she discovered about him. And she liked what she was finding. Behind that devil-may-care attitude, he was the kind of guy who liked to have fun and respected others. He'd respected her decisions and let her make the first move. Respect was something Jason had never had. Certainly not for her anyway.

And if she wasn't careful, she could easily let herself be fooled into naïvely thinking Jett felt the same way she did. Just because they'd had great sex.

Except for her, the sex was only part of it. But it would be a fatal mistake to make more of this than what it was. A one-nighter. A fling. The knowledge that she'd know her future within weeks had given her the impetus to grab tonight and make some memories.

But no matter what future she was dealt, she didn't want a man and the complications that came with him. She had too many other commitments. Others were counting on her. So staying here snuggled up next to him was a *bad* idea. She shifted experimentally. If she could just extricate herself…

'Where do you think you're going?' a surprisingly wide-awake voice muttered next to her ear.

'Down to my room,' she whispered. 'Go back to sleep.'

'Like hell you are. And I wasn't asleep.'

'Oh.' She tried again to ease away but her leg remained trapped. 'I didn't bring anything with me.'

'You brought the important stuff.' A firm arm reached

around her waist and pulled her back until she was flush against him. He was hard and erect against her bottom and obviously ready to go again.

'Tell me about this idiot boyfriend,' he murmured against her ear.

'He doesn't exist any more. Not to me.'

'How old were you?'

'Eighteen.'

'No other boyfriends?'

'I went out with a few guys in high school, but they were mostly platonic, study buddies—that kind of thing. Nerds, you'd probably say. Then I met Jason, who wasn't a nerd by any stretch of the imagination. Our relationship was a bit like a cheap sky show. Bright sparks that fizzled fast.'

'That's all? Just a spark and fizzle?'

She remembered the way things had ended. 'So after the underwhelming experience, I decided I wasn't missing much. And I was studying—I didn't have time for guys. I should go...'

'Why?' His hand slid round and found a nipple to play with. 'Stay.'

And she couldn't think of a reason why she shouldn't. Didn't really want to because *she didn't want the night to end.* 'Since we're both awake...' She turned over so they were face to face and stared into his eyes and saw her desire reflected back. 'Want to play again?'

He grinned, teeth white, eyes laughing in the dimness. 'I'm ready if you are.'

She traced the curve of his lips with a fingertip and grinned back. 'I know.'

'My turn on top,' he said, and rolled her onto her back.

CHAPTER TEN

JETT WATCHED THE SKY turn grey and the first hints of dawn creep through the shutters. The sleeping form outlined beside him snuffled and shifted but remained asleep. A grin hooked the corner of his mouth. Who'd have thunk it? Olivia snored like a trooper.

He watched her face in the pearlescent light and was tempted to wake her with a kiss on those plump and pretty lips and have his way with her again. Something powerful and almost possessive snagged in his chest. He'd had beautiful women, experienced women with all the right moves, but none of them had seduced him the way Olivia had. She'd not only seduced his body, but also his mind, with her intelligence and humour and a stubborn determination to rival his own.

He gritted his teeth against such feelings. He'd sailed on her boat as she'd requested of him, suffered his bit for charity and was leaving this morning.

Just because they'd shared a bed, a few truths and something less substantial that he hadn't quite figured out yet, didn't mean he was going to change his plans. She knew he was leaving and she had her own career path mapped out. They both understood where the other was coming from.

He was up and showered and dressed before she woke. He ordered breakfast for two then checked his emails. He had the morning sorted. They'd share coffee and croissants before they parted ways. He'd offer any further assistance for her foundation should she need it, then his chauffeured ride would drop her home if she wanted before taking him on up to Cradle Mountain. He figured he'd enjoy the scenery along the way while he jumped on the Internet and got a head start on some foody ideas during the four-hour journey...

Except he'd got used to having her around over the past week. Her boundless energy and enthusiasm was contagious, giving a much-needed boost to his flagging motivation and lack of direction of late. The way her eyes flashed when she was angry or bewildered with him. When she smiled in his direction and made his heart pound a little bit harder.

Should he ask her to come with him? Just for a couple of days? Just until this spark lost its sparkle?

He scowled at his laptop screen. Him and his sister's best friend. Yeah, right. When the spark lost its sparkle it could all get *very* messy.

He was still scowling when the tousle-haired beauty walked into the room. Wearing last night's discarded silk shirt. The top two buttons were undone, leaving a generously exposed cleavage. Its hem barely covered enough thigh to be decent; her legs flashed honey-gold in the sun's early morning glow.

'Someone went clubbing last night,' she said, fiddling with the cuffs.

'I went to check out the casino earlier in the evening.'

'I've never been to a casino, but I've heard it's fun.'

'Never made it. Wasn't in the right mood.'

'Oh. Lucky for me.' She smiled, looking sexy and adorable, and his body throbbed to instant attention. He wanted to have her here, now, and to hell with breakfast and his plans. 'There's a hotel robe in the bathroom that might be warmer,' he suggested, tearing his gaze away and returning his focus to his PC.

'I'm not cold.' She'd moved in record time because an arm shot across his line of vision. 'See, no goose-bumps.'

He nodded, resumed tapping keys. 'Just finishing something here…' She smelled of warm, musky, satisfied woman and he couldn't help it—he filled his lungs with her scent.

'You're supposed to say it looks better on me than on you.'

He'd heard that cajoling feminine tone before, just not from Olivia. He spared a glance. Beaded nipples clearly outlined against the fine fabric. He knew they were the colour of coral and tasted like mulled wine. His eyes lingered longer than he'd intended. He could feel his blood pressure rise. And other parts. This wasn't going the way he'd planned. 'So it does. Keep it if you want.' He doubted he'd wear it again—he didn't keep mementos.

To his surprise, she agreed, 'No reminders,' then reached for last night's goody bag. 'We didn't get to eat the food I brought over.' From the corner of his eye he saw her pinch off a grape and hold it out to him. 'Hungry?'

He looked up and met pretty sea-blue eyes. Yes, he was, but not for food. 'I've ordered breakfast for…' he checked the time '…fifteen minutes.'

'So we have fifteen minutes.' Popping the grape in her mouth, she started unbuttoning the shirt in a brisk, businesslike fashion.

When he watched in disbelief, she shrugged, slipping another button free, her eyes twinkling like jewels. 'Once more for the road?'

He pushed back from the table, already pulling his shirt over his head, not bothering with buttons. 'You're trouble, you know that?'

'So you've said.' She pulled a foil packet out of the shirt

pocket before she let the garment slither off those elegant creamy shoulders and onto the floor. 'More than once. I—'

He'd grabbed her around the waist, swung her up, hoisted her onto the table and spread her thighs apart before either of them knew what he was about. A glass table arrangement rocked unsteadily behind her.

He paused for a second, stunned. Something that looked like panicked excitement streaked across her gaze.

'Don't stop.'

'Don't intend to.' He slid one finger inside her.

Her gasp fired his blood to fever pitch. Snatching the condom from her fingers, he fumbled as he rolled it on then dragged her buttocks to the edge of the table. Craving the clench of her hot wet heat around him. Craving that one last time, the way an addict craved his last fix before rehab.

She leaned back on her elbows, offering. Demanding. 'Yes! Hurry.'

His vision hazed, his body shuddered, and he heard himself swear once, violently, before he leaned over her, lowered his body to hers and plunged inside. The impact drove the air from both their lungs.

'Jett!'

It wasn't pain he heard in her breathless plea. It was the same urgency that beat through his own blood. His name on her lips, over and over, her hands barely clinging to his sweat-damp shoulders, hips arching to meet his thrusts.

No slow and gentle this morning, his control was in tatters, and, he knew by looking into her eyes, she didn't want it. She wanted fast, uninhibited abandon. That was what he gave her and what she gave in return.

Sheer mindless passion. Frantic mouths and muttered pleasure. Flesh met flesh, every harsh breath expelled matched the fierce pace they'd set.

She gave him everything without fear or hesitation, eager

for more, as if she'd never get enough, her whole body vibrant and alive, her face aglow.

*As if she was trying to live an entire life in these few
crazy moments.*

He drove her up, higher, faster. The room around them
blurred, lightning cracked and they flew together through
the eye of the storm.

Olivia collapsed against the table, its glass surface cool
against her damp back. Jett's body on hers was a still-
unfamiliar and exciting weight, their sweat-slicked skin
fused together in interesting places. She wondered if she'd
find the strength to move before breakfast arrived.

He peeled himself off her, the sticky pull bringing a smile
to her numb lips. He didn't speak when he lifted her off the
table except to order her to 'Stay there,' and disappeared
into the bathroom.

She picked the silk shirt up off the floor, brought it to her
nose. His musky scent mingled with her own. *No reminders.*

She set it atop his packed bag, her mind still spinning,
her legs still shaking. Who'd have thought sex could be like
this? Not only the physical experience but the—she searched
for a word—connection.

Had her life been different and if she hadn't applied her
days and nights to the challenges of study and founding
Snowflake with such dedication, maybe she'd have had more
opportunities like this one.

But it would have been a waste. Because no one would
ever do it for her like Jett.

No reminders? *Huh.* Maybe not tangible mementos but
the memories were going to live on for a very long time. She
was *so* going to pay for this one night.

Jett appeared, still bare-chested and holding the fluffy
robe he'd mentioned. He didn't come close and slip it around
her shoulders as she half expected and fully hoped, but held

it out at arm's length. His eyes were dark and unreadable, giving her no clue how he felt. 'You okay?'

'Yes.' She took it from his hands. *It's over, Olivia. Pull yourself together and smile.*

It was a waste of a smile because she watched him shut his laptop, stow it in a briefcase beside his luggage. Not looking at her. All cool business. As if they hadn't just had wild animal sex on the table.

'Breakfast's late,' he muttered. As if he was in a hurry to get going and its tardy delivery was holding him up.

'Just as well, don't you think?'

She didn't know if he even heard. He seemed preoccupied. Almost on autopilot he reached down and swiped up the cotton shirt he'd whipped off earlier in his frenzy to have her and began undoing the buttons.

Desperation seized her. She wanted him to answer her, to notice her. To look at her the way he'd looked at her moments ago. 'Thanks for that,' she said, faking casual, glancing at the table still smeared with their skin prints.

No response.

'With everything so busy, who knows when I'll get lucky again.'

That got his attention.

What the...? Jett's gaze snapped to Olivia as she pulled the robe's tie firmly at her waist, swamping her in white terry towelling. He took a moment to process her words. Before he could draw breath, she beat him to it.

'Careful what you say, Jett, your sexist streak isn't going to impress me.'

He frowned, dumbfounded with the strange look in her eyes and her throwaway attitude. *Getting lucky.* He'd used the words himself more times than he could count. Some deep-down, primitive *possessive* part of him wanted to roar. He bunched the shirt in his fists before tossing it onto the sofa. 'Nothing to say.' Except, 'Just don't let anyone take advantage of you.'

Because he knew she was inexperienced and vulnerable and he couldn't stomach the idea of another Jason using her for all the wrong reasons.

'I've been practically celibate for twenty-six years—you don't think I know how to say no?' She pointed an accusing finger in his direction. 'Has it occurred to you that *you* took advantage on Christmas Eve? If Brie hadn't rung when she did… Think about it.'

'You'd have said yes.'

She rolled her eyes. 'Re-a-lly.'

'You wouldn't have been able to stop yourself.'

'Right,' she scoffed.

'Because we're good together, dammit. And you know it. You let me take advantage. You were *begging* me to take advantage.'

She shook her head. He watched her pace away and wanted to take her in his arms and hold her close and… And what? For God's sake. He drew in a slow, deep breath and somehow reined in his frustration.

'Okay, I admit it,' she said. 'You were different—*are* different. When I saw you I'd never felt that way before. Like I was shivery and melty at the same time. Like I was in a storm at sea with a broken mast.

'But none of that matters because I've no intention of having sex with you again, Jett. Next time we meet it'll be as friends. When Brie's there. Because one thing I sincerely hope is that this thing between us won't spoil what you and Brie have—family.'

Her absolute conviction in what she was saying riveted him to the spot. She infatuated him. That combination of strength and tenderness and understanding.

Breakfast interrupted anything he might have said and

while he signed for it and the staff set it up on a wrought-iron table in a corner overlooking the marina, Olivia grabbed her clothes and the handbag she'd left on the table and slipped from the room to shower.

Jett shrugged into his wrinkled shirt, poured coffee for them both and watched a few New Year stragglers down on the docks looking much the worse for wear while he waited for her.

He should be relieved. She wasn't some clingy female who demanded more than he wanted to give. He shook his head. Didn't mean he couldn't still ask her to accompany him to the mountains for a few days. He could talk her round. He could change her mind.

When Olivia didn't show after five minutes, he drank his coffee and broke open a croissant. He'd heard the shower switch off, but the women he knew spent an inordinate time in front of the mirror.

A few minutes later he heard her muffled voice through the closed bedroom door and got up and went to investigate. She sounded agitated but he wasn't about to eavesdrop on a private conversation. He tapped on the door. 'Everything okay in there?'

Instant silence, followed by a muffled 'I'll be there soon.'

Frowning, he returned to the table, poured himself another coffee, then dialled Room Service for a fresh pot.

She entered the room, dressed in last night's clothes, her bag slung over her shoulder, scrolling over the screen on her phone as she hurried to where she'd left her shoes and slipped them on. She didn't even glance his way. 'I can't stay for breakfast. I have to leave.'

He'd said the same often enough when *he'd* been the one rushing out after a night of casual sex. He raised his china cup towards her. 'Not even for coffee? I ordered another pot.'

She didn't answer; perhaps she hadn't heard him because she was busy digging around in her bag. 'Crap!'

He flicked her a look. 'Problem?'

She shook her head, still preoccupied with finding whatever she was searching for. 'Nothing for you to worry about.' She finally pulled out a set of keys, then put them back for no reason he could work out other than she was checking she had them. 'I hope you enjoy Freycinet Lodge.'

'Cradle Mountain. And I was thinking, if you—'

Eyes narrowed, he stepped closer and got his first good look since she'd come into the room. Her face was the colour of porridge. 'You said you were fine.'

She saw him looking at her trembling hands and clenched her fingers around her bag strap. 'I have to go.'

'Something's wrong.'

She waved him off and headed to the door. 'It's none of your concern.'

He slammed his mug down and walked towards her. 'I'm making it my concern.'

She kept her back towards him. 'I've got a cab waiting downstairs. I have to get home.'

Grabbing her arm, he swung her around. 'I'm not letting you out of here until you tell me.' Beneath his hand he could feel tremors running like quicksilver through muscle.

Her shoulders sagged, she closed her eyes briefly then stared up at him. They were dry and alarmingly devastated. 'My home's been broken into. The police tried to contact me last night and I didn't answer my mobile because I'd switched it off so they tried my room but I wasn't there because I was here. I've been making arrangements.'

He swore under his breath. 'Slow down. Take a breather.'

She thumped a fist against her thigh. 'Yeah? Your house hasn't just been burgled.'

He firmed his hold, said, 'What can I do?'

She shook her head. 'I'll contact you...some time.'

He didn't let go. 'What's the damage?'

'A security guy's meeting me there in forty-five minutes.'

'Did you have deadlocks?'

She glared at him. 'What do you think? And yes, the alarm was *on*.'

'Have you spoken with Breanna? I'll call her for you.'

'No, you will *not*. I don't want to spoil her holiday. And phone coverage is hit and miss up there. There's nothing she can do—'

'But I can.' Panicked eyes blinked at him. 'We can stand here wasting time or you can give in now, because I'm coming with you. End. Of. Discussion.'

CHAPTER ELEVEN

OLIVIA ACCEDED WITH a nod and Jett eased up a bit and released his hold. 'I've got a car waiting, I'll have it brought round.'

It was a simple matter to collect his gear and ride down the elevator, send her cab off, explain to his driver there'd been a change in plans and check them both out while she threw her stuff together. They were on their way in less than ten minutes.

He watched her stare straight ahead as they drove the short distance down the coast. She didn't even drink the take-away coffee he'd bought her while she'd been packing her things.

'I should've gone straight home after the race but I wanted to unwind in the city for New Year after all the work.'

'Why are you blaming yourself?'

'I keep thinking I must have missed something.'

'We'll know soon. Try to relax.'

She turned silent again but a short time later, her hand slammed against her throat. 'Turn here.'

He followed her gaze to a magnificent old home almost hidden by trees. They passed through tall iron gates and followed a long driveway to the house. Peeling garden gnomes and fairy statues played hide and seek amongst the foliage along the way.

A vast red-brick and cream lattice structure that might have come straight out of a luxury living magazine once upon a time came into view.

A guy in a car got out as they pulled up near the back entrance.

'Wait here,' Olivia told Jett firmly. 'I want to do this on my own.' She climbed out and the guy met her a few metres away. They walked to the back porch then disappeared inside.

Jett unloaded their bags, told the driver he'd be in contact, then looked about him as the car drove away. Fantastic views of the River Derwent, garden and natural bushland surrounded the property.

With Olivia still busy inside, Jett followed the scents of lavender and basil to a lovingly tended herb and vegetable garden. Organic, no doubt. Further on, he saw a pool, drained of water, the overhead glass structure grimy and cracked. A gazebo overgrown with weeds. The garden unkempt and parched. He'd have liked to have seen this place in its glory days.

With some physical effort and a sizeable injection of funds this place could be great again.

This place could be the retreat Olivia envisioned.

Right here. Her own home. Had she even thought of that? Excitement tingled along his nerve-endings. A new project, something different that he could really put his back into. Literally. He'd be doing something worthwhile. And at the end he could walk away with an honourable sense of achievement.

He heard the security guy's car leaving, and, following the sound, he retraced his steps through the bushland at the far edge of the property. As the house came into view he saw Olivia standing in the doorway surrounded by their luggage, hugging her upper arms, and scouring the grounds for him.

Such an unexpectedly domestic scene with the potted geraniums by her feet, her sun-stroked hair moving gently in the breeze, copper glinting amongst the red. She turned his way as if by instinct and their eyes met the way they had that first time.

And something huge swelled up inside his chest and rolled through him like one of those waves he'd experienced on *Chasing Dawn*, leaving an ache to settle uncomfortably in the hollow left behind.

He wanted to run the rest of the way, wrap his arms around her and tell her everything would be okay, but he knew she wouldn't welcome it. Not Ms Olivia Wishart, equal rights champion and feminist extraordinaire.

Olivia watched Jett's approach and she wanted to cry and be weak and female. She wanted to run to him and, just once, have someone be there for her. To have him wrap her up tightly and tell her everything would be okay. To feel safe.

But he wasn't that kind of a guy. Not Jett Davies, good-time guy and playboy.

And yet... For a moment there, she thought she'd seen... something in those deep chocolate eyes.

Probably the sun playing tricks. Blinking back those stupid female tears, she grabbed her bag and marched back inside as fast as its wheels would go. She made it to the kitchen before his hand on her shoulder stopped her.

'Whoa, slow down a minute. You'll give yourself a heart attack.'

His voice, low and steady and rational right when she needed it to be.

His aftershave reminded her that less than an hour ago they'd been lovers but he was here for her now as a support person. A friend.

His hand. Grounding her in reality.

Again she fought that urge to cling to someone strong and solid and trustworthy in a world where faceless people could take away or destroy your precious possessions and leave you feeling lost and empty and abused. She knew possessions counted for little but it didn't make it less painful.

'They knew what they were doing,' she said, turning to the window. Even the stunning coastline view failed to lift her. 'Professionals. They bypassed the security code then helped themselves. Not satisfied with that, they vandalised.' Violated her private stuff. She bit her lip, her stomach churning with so much *more* than anger. 'Who'd do that?'

'Scumbags, lowlifes. They're everywhere.'

'My bedroom.' Her lip trembled. 'They tipped out my drawers and...'

'We can fix it, skipper.'

His voice was so gentle she wanted to cry. Pride stopped her. 'Not all of it. My mother's heirloom jewellery. And I'll never be able to sleep in my room again.'

'Okay, maybe not all of it,' he agreed. 'Why don't you show me?' Still in that voice she'd barely heard from him until last night in his bed when she'd seen a side of him she'd not expected.

She led the way to her room, picked up the broken remains of an antique china ornament that had belonged to her grandmother. 'It's all so senseless.'

'Damn right.'

A chill shuddered through her. His arms came around her and this time she allowed herself to lean back and absorb a little of his strength.

'It'll be okay,' he said, combing gentle fingers through her hair. 'And you're not alone. I'm here.'

A comfort for now but so temporary. Maybe she could stay at Brie's for a while—she knew she'd be welcome—except she also knew she'd be intruding on her friend's busy social life, and late-night partying wasn't Olivia's thing. Meanwhile, 'I'll manage. They're not beating me.'

'Good girl,' he said, stepping away and pulling out his phone. 'You'll need help to clean up this mess. Do you know anyone?'

She shook her head. 'Don't worry about it. I'll do it myself.'

'Okay, then. I'll help.'

'No. I'll be fine. You should go.'

He frowned at her. 'Why do you feel you have to do this on your own? Is it because I'm a male? A chauvinistic jerk? You want to prove a point? What?'

'Cradle Mountain's waiting, remember?' Her only experiences with men had taught her that when the going got tough, the tough got going. All the way to Trinidad—or wherever it was her father had escaped to.

'You think I'd just walk away and leave you to it?' He took her hand in his big comforting one and led her down the hall and into the living room, pushed her gently into one of the overstuffed armchairs. He squatted down in front of her so that their gazes were level. Equals. 'Come on, skipper, talk to me.'

She understood now that she'd been basing her perception of men and their inability to stay and face the bad with the good on one man: her father. She'd not had many other male role models in her life to compare. Except Brie's father, who'd walked away from Jett's mother and his own son because it was all too complicated. Both had been selfish men who lacked responsibility and honour and common decency.

'I'm used to being independent,' she said. 'It's hard to be anything else.'

'We're the same in a lot of ways, you and me. We both value responsibility and achievement and independence.

Maybe we could try trusting each other more, leaning on each other a little, and see where it takes us?'

She nodded once. 'And just so you know, you're not a jerk.'

He laughed, a full belly laugh that rolled over her like velvet and relieved some of her tension, then kissed her full on the mouth. 'Don't ever change.'

'I don't intend to. I'm okay with who I am.'

'I'm okay with who you are too. I like that you can turn bad into good—Pink Snowflake's testimony to that. Let me stay for a bit and help you out here. Just temporary, until things are back to normal. It's New Year—hard to get trades-people in when everyone's on holiday.'

His words sent warmth blooming across her cheeks and inside her chest. She was unaccustomed to acceptance and approval. Guys, even other girls, saw her as a nerdy, intro-spective individual with more qualifications than she knew what to do with. Jett didn't seem bothered. 'But what about Cradle Mountain?'

'It's not going anywhere.'

'I don't want to interfere with your writing.'

'To tell you the truth, I'm not in a hurry.'

She nodded. 'Thank you.'

'You're welcome.' He rose and straightened, rubbed his hands together. 'Let's get started.'

They worked the rest of the day, only stopping for a quick bite for lunch cobbled together from what she found in the pantry and freezer. They finished the meal with slices of the Christmas cake Brie had baked for Jett.

It was hard. Heartbreaking. But Jett's company and sup-port went a long way to making it more bearable. Guys turned up to install a new security system. Late in the af-ternoon, Jett drove her car to the local shopping centre and bought ingredients for a creamy soup and pasta sauce and raspberry ripple ice cream. He added a DVD for later.

And a *food processor*.

'You might like to try it some time,' he suggested, setting it on her kitchen bench.

Where it would likely stay unopened in its box until hell froze over.

Jett asked about her house over fettuccini and a glass of red wine.

'Unfortunately, it's been let go,' she told him. 'I'm going to have to sell it and settle for sleeping on Brie's couch before we can even think of buying the land for our retreat and I know I'm going to have to settle for less than it's worth.'

He chewed for a few moments in silence, then said, 'This place means a lot to you.'

'It's home. The only one I've ever had.'

The look in his eyes told her he'd probably never called anywhere home but he could appreciate how it must feel.

'There are memories here. Happy, sad.' She took a mouthful of wine, nostalgia blurring her vision. 'I'd hang on to it if I could, but I have to be practical, not sentimental. The retreat's more important.'

He topped up their glasses. 'What are you looking for in a retreat?'

She blinked away old wishes. 'Something close to the city but not too close. With shrubbery. And a water view. Vacant blocks are hard to find. We're looking at those prefab kit homes that stack together, so it can grow as we do.'

'Have you ever thought of using this place?'

She chased the fettuccini around her plate with her fork. 'It's too small for what I have in mind and there's too much to do. We'd never be able to afford it. Have you *seen* the back yard? It's not been touched in years. The cost for that alone would be astronomical. We need to start modestly.'

He eyed her over his glass then set it down. 'I *have* seen the back yard. As a matter of fact I've had a second look. The potential's amazing. Think indoor heated pool and hot tub joined to the main house through a glass-covered walkway lined with luscious plants. You have all the basic ingredients, they just need to be used in a new way. You can create new memories to add to the old.'

She could imagine his idea, so tantalisingly real; she could almost feel the sunshine and water on her skin, could almost smell the tropical blooms. An all-weather paradise to lift flagging spirits.

For a wealthy chef with money to burn it might be a possibility, but for her it wasn't realistic. 'When I win the lottery.' She gave a half-laugh.

'You never know when your lucky numbers might come up.'

'Yeah, right, with the way my luck's going?' She deliberately switched topics. 'How about some ice cream and that DVD?' It was on the table and she flipped it over. '*Pretty Woman*? You got me a chick flick?'

He raised his glass. 'The title got me. There's one more thing.' He watched her over the rim. 'Where do the two of us go from here? Are we friends or lovers?'

Simple question, difficult answer. 'I know we're friends...' She met his full-on intensity with an intense gaze of her own. 'Everything's so complicated right now.'

He nodded, his expression unchanging. 'Friends, then.'

He'd agreed with her. No talking her into something she wasn't sure of. No trying to change her mind.

The way he'd not tried to change her mind on that last night aboard the yacht when she'd told him the same thing. He obviously respected the decisions she made.

She had to admire that.

* * *

Olivia woke next morning with a breathless gasp and yesterday's nightmare came crashing back. The last thing she remembered was the movie's opening credits. On the floor beside the sofa and his open laptop, Jett was surfacing too.

'Morning,' she murmured, staring into his dark, sleepy eyes. 'Sorry. I fell asleep.' Obviously. 'Why didn't you use one of the bedrooms?'

He blinked awake. 'Was awake till four working on a few ideas.' He stretched, looking gorgeously rumpled and sexy, darkly stubbled and bleary-eyed.

'Ideas? For your book?'

'Nope.' He leaned back against the sofa and watched her. 'We'll talk about it later.'

She was ultra-aware that yesterday morning's love-in was an unspoken conversation between them. She wanted, so badly, to slide down onto the floor and join him. Join *with* him. *Look away, Olivia.*

She pushed back the throw Jett must have covered her with and stood, still in yesterday's clothes and looking like something the cat had dragged in. 'I'll see what I can find for breakfast,' she said, and hurried to the kitchen.

Leaning on the open fridge door, she told herself she could come up with a cooked breakfast. She never bothered but Jett would want something.

And he was going to discover very quickly how limited her cooking skills were. She lived largely on a diet of healthy raw foods—often by necessity—but she could cook the basics. Very basic. Having a personal chef around twenty-four-seven for the next few days could prove a blessing. Or not.

'You go shower. I'll get breakfast,' Jett said, behind her, relieving her of the problem of how he wanted his eggs cooked and whether he was going to watch.

Maybe he'd already picked up on her lack of expertise.

Or he couldn't bear to look at her in her state of dishabille. Either way, she escaped without putting up much of a fight.

A short time later, feeling refreshed and towelling her damp hair, she followed the aromas of grilled bacon and coffee.

'Smells fantastic.'

When he saw her, he slid food onto two plates. 'Sit down and eat while I talk.'

She did as he told her. He didn't mean to come across so dictatorial. Since Jason, she'd never imagined feeling comfortable with a man who seemed to dominate everyone around him but Jett was different. Unlike Jason, she knew he'd at least listen. Also unlike Jason, with Jett she felt safe. And respected.

'I did some costing while you were asleep last night.' He set her plate in front of her, sat down opposite with his own. 'Ran a few ideas by an architect I know. With thought and planning we could turn this place into your retreat.'

'Jett...no.' She shook her head. 'I told you. An architect?' She didn't like that he was way ahead of her. 'Too expensive. You—'

'Hear me out. Just close your eyes and visualise. Please.'

'Okay, but this is *my* baby.'

'Goes without saying,' he reassured her. 'But it doesn't hurt to have another person's take on it.'

She closed her eyes.

'Improve and extend the kitchen garden so that in time, when the facility opens, it'll supply its own organic produce. Upgrade the pool facilities to include a relaxing fitness area and equipped gymnasium and join it to the main building. We knock down walls and extend the back of the house into—'

'Whoa.' She shook her head, her mind spinning. 'Even with the money we raised on *Chasing Dawn*, we'd only manage a fraction of that. We should rename her *Chasing Dreams*.'

He nodded. 'Why don't you? Sounds appropriate.'

'Because I'm going to sell her.' Her decision wasn't one she'd made lightly.

He frowned. 'Doesn't she hold special meaning for you and your mother?'

'She's done her job. I need the money for other things,' she said briskly, dropping her gaze to her plate.

'I've been looking for a new project,' he told her slowly. 'I'd like to work with you on this. You and my sister are in this together, which kind of gives me a foot in the door, wouldn't you say?'

'But what about your cookbook plans?' Your *life*?

'At the moment this is right where I want to be—working on something different. I'll still write but I'd like to be involved in this venture.'

She tempered the rising excitement; there was the complication of their relationship to consider, but she was thinking... Having him aboard had so many advantages. Brie could get to know her brother better. Jett would have his opportunity to look at something new. He'd bring a different perspective to the table.

She'd get to see more of him.

'I'll have to talk to Brie,' she said.

'That's all I ask. If you're both fine with it, do we have a deal?'

She agreed and they took their coffee outside so he could show her how some of his ideas might work around the property.

Jett watched her eyes light up at his suggestions. Her response further fired his excitement. But excitement of a different kind wasn't happening. *I've no intention of having sex with you again, Jett.*

He knew time and circumstances weren't favourable to revisit that particular conversation. More importantly, maybe she'd be willing to accept his support for now without the complication of sex getting in the way.

And he had a plan to make her smile again.

CHAPTER TWELVE

THAT EVENING, over the steaks he'd slapped on the grill while Olivia caught up on insurance claims and financial matters, Jett told her to keep the following day free.

'I can't just take the day off,' she told him in shock-horror and set down her cutlery with a sharp clink. 'You've seen this place.'

'Which is why I've arranged to fly my housekeeper over.'

Her brows rose into her hair. 'Fly her from Melbourne?'

'An hour's flying time away and she's excited about spending some time in Hobart. She's going to spend the day tidying up at your place then stay overnight with an old friend.'

'You've already asked her? Without speaking to me first?'

'I talked to her last night when I was making arrangements; you were asleep. I trust her. You can too.'

'I didn't think you trusted people.'

'I trust Emily Branson. She's a fifty-year-old church-going grandmother. Listen,' he continued when he saw a protest forming on her lips. 'Do *you* trust *me*?'

'Doesn't mean I go along with your plans like I don't have a will of my own. Or a brain. Okay, Emily can—'

'I've also made other plans for tomorrow.'

Watching him carefully, she nibbled on a piece of bacon. 'What kind of plans?'

'It's a surprise. But I can tell you a change of scenery and something new to think about will do you a world of good. You'll come back fresh and rejuvenated. Okay?'

She blinked several times, her eyes growing wide. 'Okay. But—'

'Pack an overnight bag—and a swimsuit—and be ready to leave at seven a.m.'

The early summer morning was clear when their small private aircraft landed at Tullamarine airport. Moments later Olivia and Jett were approaching Melbourne's CBD in a sleek red helicopter, skimming the Yarra River and landing on the helipad beside a pretty park opposite the biggest casino in the southern hemisphere.

Olivia watched the sleek skyscrapers as they travelled the short distance to their hotel within the casino complex. She'd been told to expect luxury and was enjoying every exhilarating minute, so excited she'd barely stopped to breathe. 'Where's your place? Do you live in the city?'

'See that building?' He pointed to a white tower spearing into the blue. 'Twenty-first floor. But we won't have time.'

'Oh.' Pity. His secluded world up in the sky might have given her further insight into Jett Davies but it wasn't going to happen today.

As they entered the sparkling lobby she wondered what arrangements he'd made regarding rooms but didn't have time to ask because a stylish woman in her mid-thirties wearing a trim white pant-suit with a multi-hued scarf was approaching with a smile on her glossed lips.

'Jett. Good morning.'

'Tyler.' He brushed a kiss over her cheek. 'Long time no see,' he said, then touched Olivia's shoulder briefly. 'I'd like you to meet Olivia.'

'Welcome to Melbourne, Olivia.' Her handshake was brisk and businesslike. 'Smooth flight over?'

'Thanks, Tyler, and yes, smooth as silk.'

'Jett told me it's a day of surprises, so if you're wondering what's next, say goodbye to him for now. I'm going to be your personal shopper for the next two and a half hours and we're going to have a *Pretty Woman* shopping spree in some of Melbourne's famous boutiques.'

She grinned. 'Sounds awesome.'

'Before you go,' Jett said, holding his hand out, palm up, 'your credit cards stay with me until tomorrow.'

'But—'

'Shopping time's ticking. The whole purse. Now.'

Knowing he meant it, that he wanted to do this for her no strings attached, Olivia met his eyes as she handed it over, mouthing, *'Thank you.'* She wanted to stop a moment and tell him how much she appreciated everything but Tyler was already moving off so she settled for a finger wave and a smile she couldn't have wiped away if she'd tried. 'Bye.'

She fell in love with Melbourne's quaint little arcades, Victorian architecture and exclusive boutiques. Tyler informed Olivia she was to purchase something sophisticated for the evening. Anything else she fancied was up to her.

They browsed designer wear. Metallic, silk, subtle, bold. Backless, one-sleeved, split thigh. 'What colour does he like?' Olivia wondered.

'He loves your hair. So earthy colours that bring out its beauty.' She pulled out an unusual metallic olive-green dress with a sheer bodice insert studded with tiny gold beads and held it up. 'Try this, see what you think.'

He'd told this woman he loved her hair? He'd never told *her* he loved her hair. She felt a warm glow inside her chest as she studied Tyler's choice. 'The colour's great, unusual, but the neckline's way too daring, even with the insert.'

'I guarantee you'll love it.'

'You know Jett personally,' she said, slipping it on. None of Olivia's business but she wondered if Jett and the striking blonde had been lovers.

'I took one of his cooking courses in France a few years ago when I was on vacation. I owned a little café here in Melbourne at the time and we stayed in touch. Oh, my.' She clasped her hands under her chin. 'That looks stunning on you. And it fits like a glove. Trust me, it's Jett's kind of dress.'

So she knew him *that* well? Olivia would never have chosen it but she had to agree, the gown looked amazing. And how long had it been since she'd spent anything on herself? Not that she was the one spending... The sunburst of beads flowed from the sheer bodice and down over one hip. And if the neckline practically plunged to her navel, so what? It had inbuilt support and this might be the last time she got to show off her cleavage.

She hadn't realised she needed this day until now. More, Jett had anticipated exactly what she wanted. Obviously Jett understood women. He knew what they liked, knew how to please them.

'I'll take it,' she decided.

Olivia managed to purchase some pretty underwear and a couple of outfits before time was up.

'Jett and I saw quite a bit of each other while I was in France,' Tyler said as the car drove them towards the hotel. She glanced Olivia's way, obviously reading her mind. 'I'd be curious too, if I was you.'

'No. No.' *I'm not curious.* 'We...he...' Olivia tripped over her own tongue. 'Jett and I aren't in a relationship.'

'There were some moments with Jett and me, but in the end we settled for friends.'

'And that's what we are. Just friends.'

'Olivia,' she said, shaking her head, a small smile on her lips. 'I've seen you two together for less than two minutes and I can tell you "just friends" is something you and he will never be.'

No time to protest because the car was already drawing up at the lobby. A porter collected her shopping bags, Tyler said goodbye and Jett climbed in.

Their chocoholic tour lasted over an hour, starting with a French morning tea and cake in a little café while they learned about chocolate making with a small group of other tourists.

Finally, wondering if she'd still fit into her new dress, Olivia had a chance to see her hotel room when she went upstairs to freshen up and find her swimsuit. The first things she'd noticed were the two queen beds but she didn't see Jett's bag. She reminded herself it was her choice to remain friends.

She stood a few moments alone, soaking in the floor-to-ceiling view of Melbourne and the casino and catching her breath. Her life seemed a world away. Her problems non-existent for now. This was a day in a million and she intended to make the most of it.

They spent the latter part of the afternoon in the fitness centre. Lazed in the infinity pool overlooking the city. They weren't alone—it was holiday season after all—but their interaction was companionable. Jett kept her focus on other topics—places they'd travelled, movies they'd seen, their tastes in music. Recognising him, a couple of women exchanged glances and watched with lust-envy as he rose from the pool, water sluicing off the hard planes of his body, his swimming trunks clinging to his powerful thighs.

Olivia knew how they felt and was relieved Jett had organised an aromatherapy massage for her. It helped iron out the kinks stress had brought on over the past couple of days.

But it didn't take her mind off Jett's near-naked body not far away. Nor did it stop her from imagining stripping off his swimmers and having her way with him on his lounger.

He was still stretched out on that lounger pecking away on his laptop when she returned. She drew in a deep breath, let it out slowly, indulging in the private fantasy.

Sensing her gaze, Jett dragged his eyes away from his screen to watch Olivia in her black swimsuit, hair piled on top of her head, her skin flushed rose and glistening with body oil.

He nearly groaned aloud. His whole body tightened, his blood turned to lava and flowed thickly through his veins.

'Feeling better?' He wished to hell he did. Today had been an exercise in self-control, keeping his hands to himself and refusing to think about the bottle of French champagne he'd put in the room's bar fridge for later tonight and whether or not he was going to get the opportunity to share it with her.

'I feel *fabulous*.' She stretched her arms up, drawing his gaze to the undersides of her Lycra-clad breasts, then she seemed to remember where she was and let them drop to her sides, pronto. 'I need a shower. What time's dinner?'

'Seven. You have the room to yourself. I'll meet you in the lobby at six-fifty.' He shifted uncomfortably. 'I suggest you go now before I decide to accompany you to that shower.'

She half smiled, half...*what*? before she turned, picked up her belongings and sauntered away.

Whatever it was he'd glimpsed in her eyes, he had a good feeling that his bottle of champagne was going to taste very sweet indeed.

A punctual woman.

Of course she was. Everything in Olivia Wishart's life was organised and shipshape. He stood near the lobby windows, his body in lockdown as Olivia walked towards him.

His throat went dry as his eyes feasted on the scrumptious vision. *Thank you, Tyler.*

The metallic sheen changed from shades of blanched asparagus to aubergine to sage depending on the down-lights. It flowed to mid-calf and caressed every curve. He thought vaguely that someone had forgotten to sew in a bodice then realised it was some sort of sheer lacy stuff studded with tiny beads. What fabric there was clasped her breasts, showing them off to glorious perfection right where he wanted to put *his* hands.

She looked like a goddess and he wanted to worship at her shiny stilettoed shoes, then work his way up.

She smiled, secure in her feminine knowledge that she was making an impact. 'Good evening.'

'I reckon it is.' He took her hand. 'And it's about to get a whole lot better. We'll walk—it's not far.'

The tables were set amongst trees lit with fairy lights, the early evening summer sun glinted off nearby buildings, turning the white linen cloths gold.

Over drinks and appetisers they talked about the day. As the evening wore on and the sky turned to purple conversation turned more personal.

And he found himself telling Olivia stuff about his life, about himself. General stuff. His years in foster homes, his time as a sous chef in Paris, but he'd never opened up so candidly to anyone before. Unlike other women she didn't prod or try to get him to talk about things that made him uncomfortable and yet she was interested in what he did share.

It was later than he'd intended when they finally finished their coffee. He reached across the table, touched her hand. 'I had plans to take you to the casino in that spectacular dress and make every man there jealous that you're with me.'

Her cheeks flushed and she smiled. 'Honestly, Jett, can I take a rain check on that? I'd just like to go on up to the room.' She turned her hand over beneath his and entwined their fingers.

Her eyes met his, darkening as desire and anticipation brought a flush to her cheeks. He watched the way her lips parted ever so slightly, giving him a tiny glimpse of pink tongue.

'We can do that.'

She hesitated then said, 'I didn't notice your bag there earlier.'

'It's there now.'

Her eyes darkened. 'I'm glad.'

He smiled. *So am I.*

In the elevator with another couple they stood millimetres apart, watching the numbers light up as they ascended.

The moment they were out of the lift, he gathered her in and touched his lips to hers. 'Are we on the same page here?' he murmured against her mouth.

'Yes.' She sounded breathless.

With his hand on her back, he steered her to their room, pushed open the door and pulled her inside. No need for lighting; the glow from the city bathed the room, giving her skin a pearlescent sheen. Eyes on his, she reached up behind her neck. 'I'm going to need some help getting this dress off.'

'I was hoping you'd say that.'

He loved the sexy sound of the zip sliding down her back, the warm sensation of her smooth skin against his palm, her little shiver of delight. He drew the dress down and she stepped out of it, leaving her in nothing but lacy black panties and stilettos.

Her breasts. Plump and full and tantalising. He moulded his hands around them, taking their weight, and blew out a slow breath. 'You're the sexiest woman alive.'

'You make me feel sexy.' She undid his tie, slid it off, dropped it on the floor. 'It's a good feeling.' Tracing a fingernail down his shirt, she stopped at his belt buckle. 'I've never felt sexy the way you make me feel sexy. From the first time we met on that little balcony you've made me feel desired and all woman.' She looked up at him. 'You were a master seducer then and you're a master seducer now and I'm afraid I've fallen under your spell.'

'You're wrong,' he told her, lost for a moment in the warm sea of her eyes. 'You're the spell-weaver.'

'This—*us*—like *this*…together…isn't meant to happen.'

No, he thought. It wasn't. He hadn't expected to feel the way she made him feel. Out of control one moment, invincible the next. Right now he was more out of control than superhero.

'Don't think about tomorrow,' he told her, as much to her as to himself. 'Or next week or the week after that.' He lifted her, carried her to the nearest bed and laid her down. 'Just think about tonight.' He slipped off her shoes, set them on the floor. 'Us. Now.'

'Great idea.' She smiled, her hands sliding beneath the pillow as she blinked up at him, looking deliciously naked and drowsy.

'Wait right there,' he told her.

'Not going anywhere,' he heard her murmur as he strode to the bar fridge.

In less than a minute he'd uncorked his bottle of vintage champagne, poured two glasses. He toed off his shoes, picked up their drinks, anticipation licking along his veins. 'Don't fall asleep on me…'

Too late. He trailed off at her side of the bed. Out cold. Soft snores she'd never willingly make—or acknowledge— if she were awake, he thought, a smile twitching at the corner of his mouth. She needed the rest. As he watched her face relax and the tensions of the past couple of days fade his disappointment that the evening wasn't going to end the way he wanted it melted away, overtaken by a tenderness he'd never experienced. He pulled the sheet over her utterly tranquil body then walked to the window and watched Melbourne's traffic below.

New and unfamiliar sensations were creeping under his guard almost without his knowledge—and definitely without his permission. He never let anyone close. What was it about Olivia? She wasn't like other liaisons he'd had. She was genuine, caring, not all about a good time. She put others before herself. Her brand of sexy was natural and almost naïve, no guile, no pretence.

Moving away from the view, he tossed back the contents of his glass, then stripped down to underwear and positioned himself as far as possible on the other side of the bed. Wasn't working. He could hear her breathing. Her musky feminine scent teased him. He pounded the pillows into submission and switched the TV on to mute.

Shopping TV. The last damn thing he needed.

'Come on, skipper. Time to wake up. Olivia.'

She heard her name, felt a hand on her shoulder as she stirred into consciousness. Jett. She groaned, covering her eyes from the glare with an arm. *What was that light?* 'What's the time?'

'Eleven o'clock.'

'That's a bloody lie.'

'I wish it was,' she heard him say. 'You've slept over twelve hours.'

'It's a relief to hear that,' she muttered. 'I thought for a moment we'd made mad passionate love and I'd forgotten.'

'If we'd made mad passionate love you wouldn't have forgotten.'

'No.' Holding the sheet in front of her, she pushed up and stared into those gold-flecked eyes and wanted to scream her frustration. 'I've never fallen asleep with anyone before and I've done it twice with you.'

His lips twisted. 'Great for a guy's self-esteem.'

'If you want to know, you make me feel safe. Last night was the first time I've felt truly relaxed since the break-in. No bad dreams, nothing but calm. So thank you.' And she was refreshed and ready to get on with the day…or anything else.

'I'm glad,' he said, kissing her brow. 'But the flight leaves in ninety minutes. I tried to delay it but the aircraft's schedule is chockers.' He gestured to a breakfast tray on the table by his laptop where he'd obviously been working. 'You've got time for a quick shower and there's something to eat.'

Then she noticed he was dressed for business. 'What's happening?'

'Seems my adventure on the high seas has attracted continuing interest in the media. I've been invited to appear on the *Taste Buds and Travel* show—a traveller's guide to eating around the world.'

'I know what it is,' she said, struggling not to be disappointed because she knew immediately he wasn't returning to Hobart with her.

'I told them I'll do it for double what they're offering me.' He grinned like a kid at Christmas. 'Timing, hey?'

Yeah, she thought. *Bad* timing. But why quibble about money? Didn't he have enough already? Frowning, she reached for her bag beside the bed and began pulling out clothes. She'd never thought him money-motivated. 'It's a great publicity opportunity.' Not that he needed it. Hadn't he been *avoiding* it?

'I've arranged to go in and discuss it later this afternoon, then I'll stay at the apartment for the night.'

'Sounds exciting.' She walked towards the bathroom, annoyed with him. Annoyed with *herself* for being annoyed with him. 'Don't forget to let me know how it goes.'

'You'll be the first to know. Olivia.'

His commanding tone had her stopping despite herself. She didn't turn around. 'Yes?' She heard the bite in her own voice.

'Snowflake's the *only* reason I'm considering it.'

She turned, looked at him, confused. 'Snowflake?'

'I'll get to promote it and my appearance fee will go straight to your retreat project along with any donations the show brings in. I've told them my terms and they've agreed.'

So generous. So unexpected. She'd misjudged him too quickly. 'Thank you. I don't know what to s—'

'I'll be back in Hobart tomorrow. If you're worried, I can get Emily to stay on with you.'

Her fingers tightened on her clothes. 'No, I'll be fine. Really.'

'If you're sure.' He poured coffee and held it out.

'Later,' she said, and hurried into the bathroom. Everything would have been perfect except that he wasn't asking her to stay another night with him.

CHAPTER THIRTEEN

OLIVIA SAT AT her kitchen table, mobile pressed to her ear, listening to Jett's deep voice telling her about the highlights of his day on *Taste Buds and Travel*.

'Sounds like fun,' she said, keeping her voice bright but feeling half-hearted. Her life sounded incredibly dull in comparison. So far, with the break-in and its repercussions she'd not done much of what she'd set out to achieve on her month's leave.

And she still hadn't heard from her specialist.

Jett's overnighter had morphed into its fourth day. The producers had wanted to do the show while public interest was high, which meant he'd put everything else on hold.

'We should have a fundraiser,' he said, switching topics. She perked up. 'For Snowflake?'

'Of course for Snowflake, what else? I've got a few ideas if you're interested.'

She smiled. 'I'm interested.'

'We can discuss it when I get back tomorrow night.'

'You're done? You're coming ho—back?' Her fingers tightened on her phone. 'What time?'

'I'll be there around seven. I've got a dinner meeting with a publisher in an hour, so I have to go now but I'll see you tomorrow evening.'

Nerves did a crazy whirlpool in her tummy but her voice

was smooth sailing. 'See you then,' she said, and disconnected.

I love him. The words danced a drunken sailor's jig in
her head and her feet followed, spinning across the kitchen
floor till she bumped up against the kitchen table. She was
giddy, head-over-heels in love.

But it was her forever secret because she could never let
him know.

But she *could* let him know how grateful she was for all
he'd done for her. Her gaze fell on the food processor he'd
bought that was pushed to the far end of the table up against
the wall, still lurking in its box, waiting for her.

A challenge. She stepped over, ripped the tape off the lid
and glared at it. Not only a challenge, a distraction. She'd
show him she appreciated all he'd been doing. That she appreciated *him*. That she could cook even if it was basic. She
pulled out the shiny red machine. She'd find some simple
recipes on the Internet.

The lamb casserole was in the oven, its delicious rosemary
and garlic aroma filling the kitchen. The fruit salad was
chopped and in the fridge. The ingredients for Tassie salmon
mousse were ready to go. She'd had to dash to the shop to
buy gelatine so she was behind schedule but that was fine.
She had time—it was only five o'clock.

She added the ingredients to the new blender, covered it
with the lid, switched it on. She wrinkled her nose—salmon
sure smelled fishy. When the mixture was smooth, she un-
twisted the glass jug from its base. …Only the jug was supposed to be *lifted* off the base, not unscrewed like Brie's, she
realised too late. A tsunami of salmon mixture flooded out
of the bottom, over the new appliance, the bench, the floor.
Down her T-shirt and jeans. By the time she'd switched it
off at the wall before she electrocuted herself, it was im-

possible to screw it back on. The blender was ruined. Her hands stank.

Where was a cat when she needed one?

Eew! She was never going to eat salmon mousse again.

She was never going to cook for him again.

The sound of a car pulling up sent her rushing to the window. *Let it be the carpenter returning for his tools.* But no, Jett was unfolding his tall frame from the front passenger seat. Her heart went into overdrive.

Mr Jettsetter Chef himself.

No-o-o! This was not allowed to happen. She rinsed her salmon-stinky hands under the tap—couldn't do anything about the spatter on her T-shirt—then rushed to the door. And there he was, his stubble a tad more scruffy than usual, temptation and persuasion in his eyes.

'You're way early...' *I've missed you.* 'There's a bit of a mess...' *I've missed you more than I should have.*

The first thing Jett noticed as the door opened was the way his heart stumbled over itself at his first glimpse of red hair and blue-lagoon eyes. The second thing was the glop of something on her freckled cheek. The third was the fishy smell that wafted out with her.

'I got an earlier flight.' Because there'd been an inexplicable urgency to see her again. To watch her face light up in surprise—at least he'd hoped it would. But she looked more horrified than surprised. He reached out and flicked at the goop, sniffed.

'Oh, no.' Her cheeks turned a matching colour and she blinked at his thumb in disbelief. 'I was making salmon mousse.' She stared down at herself. 'I had an accident. Sort of.'

He licked the goop from his thumb and his gaze followed hers. 'I see. Sort of.' And it occurred to him—something that filled him with a warm, satisfied glow. 'Were you making dinner for me?'

'No big deal, is it?' She stepped back. Still her eyes didn't leave his. 'I'll go take a shower and change out of these stinky...' Her hands flapped about her. 'I'll just clean this kitchen up first... Your blender, I'm sorry...'

'Easy. It's okay. I'll get you another one.'

'Please don't.'

He laughed. He wanted to kiss her full on those passion-pink lips and drink her in, salmon smell and all. Hell, he wanted to help her out of those clothes and dive beneath that spray with her.

But the few days apart had changed the easy camaraderie they'd built between them in Melbourne and there was that awkwardness between them again. It was like starting over. 'Why don't you take that shower while I clean up here?'

'Right. Thanks. The casserole's—'

'Fine. I know.'

'Ah...yes, of course you do.' She turned and bolted.

He stared at the empty doorway. He'd never seen Olivia so flustered. It almost felt as if they were on a first date and she'd invited him for dinner but he'd turned up early. He glanced through the arch, saw the dining table covered in a lace cloth that hadn't been there before. Silverware. Miniature roses he recognised from the front garden. Five tall white candles in a bronze candelabra.

Dating. Now there was a word he hadn't associated with himself in for ever. And none of those 'dates' had ever been of the wholesome domestic home-grown variety.

Perhaps being apart wasn't so bad after all because coming back sure felt good.

Didn't mean anything, he assured himself. He was staying awhile longer and helping her out as they'd already talked about. He'd leave when things were moving along. As they'd already talked about.

A flicker of heat skimmed through his veins as he scooped up the blender, put it in the packaging it had come in to toss out later. What other surprises did she have planned for this evening? Filling the sink with soapy water, he sloshed the dishcloth over the benches.

He'd had women cook extravagant and sophisticated meals to impress, to please, to seduce him into their bed. And many had succeeded. Because he'd wanted to be impressed and seduced.

But Olivia didn't hang on his every word. In fact, she *argued* with him—long and hard. Her meal looked basic and she'd stuffed up with the salmon.

She was gorgeous, sexy, intelligent and brave.

Glad to have something useful to do while he waited, he wiped up the floor with kitchen paper towel, found a mop and bucket to finish the job.

With the kitchen restored, he set his bag in the bedroom she'd been using then sat on the edge of her bed and listened to the shower running in the en suite. He imagined her head tipped back as water splashed over her neck and darkened her hair to burgundy. Thought about that warm water sluicing over her breasts, rivulets flowing down her abdomen, collecting in her navel. And down...

The fragrance of her shower gel seeped out to flirt and lure. And before he knew it, he was tapping on the door. 'I'm going to open the door a fraction.' He yelled over the sound of the spray. 'I want you to listen to me. Okay?'

He heard nothing but water splashing on tiles and for a moment he thought she hadn't heard but then her muffled 'Okay.'

He cracked the door open and was greeted with a cloud of steam. 'Olivia.'

'When you use my name all serious like that I get worried. Is someth—?'

'Nothing's wrong. Do you trust me?'

Silence. He could hear his heart beating, the water splashing.

Finally a quiet 'Yes.'

He grinned to himself. 'I'm coming back in five minutes and I'm coming in. You can decide if you want to stay under the shower or get dressed—and if you choose the latter, *how* you dress is kind of key.'

A brief hesitation, then, 'All right.'

Olivia's pulse rate tripled and she gasped in large lungfuls of steam as the warm spray pelted her body. Her fingers curled on the gold-plated taps and the spray continued. She wasn't going anywhere.

She couldn't see him when he returned a few moments later but she saw the movement against the fogged glass.

'I'm back,' he informed her.

'So I see.' Or almost. From the looks of it, he was still wearing his jeans and black T-shirt but less than a dozen rapid heartbeats later all she could see was the nude colour of a tall male body.

She gripped the soap ledge for support. And waited.

'I need you to move so your head's not under the spray and close your eyes.'

She did as he requested and felt the draught ripple over wet skin as he opened the shower screen door. He didn't touch her but held something cold and smooth against her upper lip.

'You've brought *glass* into my shower?'

'Yes. What can you smell?'

'Alcohol. Are you planning to get me drunk?'

'A little tipsy, maybe. Alcohol,' he repeated. 'Details, please.'

A shiver of anticipation ran through her body. 'Spirits. Rum? And mint. So something cool, and possibly lethal.'

'Try it.' He tipped the glass against the seam of her mouth and she tasted a few drops on her tongue. 'What else?'

'Lime? Or lemon.'

'Good.'

She sipped again. 'It's nice. Sensual. Can I open my eyes now?'

'Not yet. Another sip. It's my Blue Mint Lagoon cocktail.'

'Ah, your specialty cocktail.' She did as he asked, taking tiny sips and letting the smooth ice-cold liquid slide down her throat. 'What else is in it?'

'I'll let you think about it. Meanwhile...' He removed the glass from her lips and she heard him set it on the vanity with a little *chink* on the marble. 'Eyes still shut, now.'

He nudged her mouth open with his thumb and slipped a cocktail-soaked strawberry between her lips. She chewed it slowly, enjoying the contrast in texture. 'Mmm, yum. Different.'

'Like you.'

She felt him move behind her into the shower stall. Its generous size accommodated two people and meant their bodies didn't touch, but she felt every single drop of water on her oversensitised skin. 'Place your palms flat on the tiles in front of you,' he told her. 'And be ready for a surprise.'

Tension built to a fever pitch, her whole body felt tight and strung out. Anticipation quivered through her. Then he stroked something cold and slippery over the back of her neck and she squealed with the sudden shock and the unexpected pleasure of hot and cold. 'Ice? What...?'

She trailed off because she was concentrating on the way the ice—in both his hands—felt, mingling with the hot spray as he stroked lower, all the way down her spine, slowing to massage a tight circle at the small of her back, then down the backs of her legs, lingering at sensitive areas behind her knees. And back up all the way to her nape.

She heard him crunch ice between his teeth then he was sucking on her shoulder, her ear lobe, her neck, with icy lips and tongue.

She thought she might melt like the ice and disappear down the drain in a mindless puddle but then he leaned close so that his body pressed against her back, a thigh between her legs to keep her in place.

His murmured 'Spread your legs for me' had her breath catching. The warm hardness of his body surrounded her while he continued to rub the slippery coldness over her nipples, making them impossibly tight and erect. Making her shiver and moan.

'Oh, my...' She squirmed back against him in delight then gasped, held her breath in awe as he pushed slowly inside her from behind. Filling her up with heat while he continued skating swirling patterns of ice over her skin. Hot and cold, slippery sensations. The squat fat candle she kept by the bath infusing the steam with an arousing and mellow scent of vanilla.

This was all about contrasts and new experiences and he'd planned it specifically for her pleasure. A quivering started low and deep in her belly and spiralled outward. The air moist and soft all around her, the torrent of water hot and stinging on her shoulders. His ice-chilled lips nuzzling her neck.

Her flesh yielding against his.

She'd always told herself she'd never give up control but it was indeed a delicious surrender.

'Lean back and hold on to the back of my neck,' he told her. Fierce, urgent, his lips moving over her shoulder. 'I want to feel you come.'

'Yes...' Flinging her arms tight around the back of his

neck, she shuddered as tremor after tremor rolled through her. She felt his own tremors, his breath harsh and fast as he climaxed inside her. And her body claimed him, her muscles clenched around him, pulling him deep inside her, touching her womb, her heart.

A short time later, as the setting summer sun painted the sky gold and crimson, they lay entwined on her bed, bodies still damp.

'It's past eight,' Olivia said lazily. 'Dinner's more than ready, if you're hungry.'

'I've got something we can enjoy first.'

'More?' She felt for him beneath the sheet. 'You really are magnificent.'

'Not quite that magnificent, for the moment at least.' Pushing up, he grinned, kissed her nose. 'Wait here.'

This time she didn't fall asleep while she waited. He returned with a drink-laden tray and a plate of strawberries. She felt like the cat who'd eaten more than her share of cream. 'More Blue Mint Lagoon cocktail?'

'I wanted you to appreciate it fully and leisurely so I made a couple of extras earlier.' He handed her one, took the other and they drank.

He swirled his glass slowly, looking at her. 'The first time I saw you it was your eyes that got my attention.'

'Not my breasts?'

'Nope—but they were a close second. I could feel those eyes on me as I came down those stairs.

'And then I saw them for the first time and they reminded me of this drink. Sea-green with that hint of cool blue lagoon and warm sandy shallows. I knew then I'd been captured.'

'By a mermaid.' She raised her glass at him again, drunk on happiness. 'Not a pirate.'

'Mermaids.' He took her glass and set it on the bedside table with his, then stretched alongside her. He cruised his fingers lightly down her belly, his gaze following his hand until they reached the top of her thighs. 'They don't have what you have.'

She grinned. 'You know, I had an erotic dream about a pirate during the race.'

He looked at her with interest. 'I hope you didn't surrender to his wicked charms.'

'Oh, but I did—Captain Jett Black, he was.'

'Ah, yes.'

Jett recalled finding her dishevelled and dispirited below decks on that last day of the race. He knew she'd been thinking about her mum because Breanna had told him. The skipper had made it clear she wanted nothing to do with him.

'You were most vehement you wanted me far, far away.'

'It was an erotic dream, Jett, of course I wanted you far, far away. How embarrassing.'

She blushed, and he grinned at her. 'You mean you were…?'

Her chin jerked upwards. 'You'll never know, Captain Black.' Then her feistiness turned mellow and she was nestling her head in his shoulder. 'Was my asking about your surname that day a problem for you?'

'No. It just brought it all back—remembering the day I met my father.'

She lifted her head to look at him, her brow creased in puzzlement. 'Brie never told me about that. She didn't even know you existed till your father died.'

'Breanna never knew. She was only a couple of months old. I was five and my mum had died a few months previously. Of a drug overdose.' He shrugged. 'Past history.'

'Jett.' She placed a warm hand on his chest, over his heart. Her gaze, so clear and honest and open. 'I think it's time you told me, don't you?'

He blew out a slow sigh, remembering the day as clear as if it had happened yesterday. 'It was Christmas Day and

I'd been taken from the foster home to meet him. A kid's dream come true. But then Breanna was there…'

She kissed the place where his messed-up heart beat strong against her cool lips, then rested her chin on his chest and waited.

'I was the unwanted result of an affair. And I resented Breanna for something she had no control over. So I made my foster families' lives hell. Pushed kids away because I didn't want to risk having them like me then turn against me because I couldn't stand the idea of being rejected again.'

'Brie doesn't know all this stuff,' Olivia said softly when he'd finished. 'She'll understand you better if you tell her.'

'I will. Soon.'

'She wants to help but doesn't know how.'

'When Breanna located me, it was a shock. Family and belonging and being close to people was new to me. Still is.'

'It destroyed her when her father came clean,' Olivia said. 'She'd lost her mother in a car accident a few years earlier. Everything she'd thought about her family was turned on its head. But she wants that connection with you. You're all she has.'

He tangled his fingers in Olivia's hair and stared into those emotion-filled eyes. 'She has you.'

'I'm not her family, Jett. She needs that family connection. And so do you.'

Her words struck deep. He wanted to tell her she was wrong but the words stuck in his throat. Because she wasn't wrong. Through her own actions, she'd demonstrated family love could be strong and committed and unconditional. And he could have that too; he just had to reach out and take it.

He continued stroking her hair. 'I'm sorry your mum passed away. You two obviously had loads in common and were very close.'

'In so many ways.' Her voice turned sadder than he'd ever

heard. Her eyes filled with clouds before she turned away to stare out at the night.

He sensed there was more she wasn't saying.

'What do you mean?' When she didn't respond, he was seized by a fierce need to know. He wanted to hold her close and demand she tell him. 'I just told you stuff I've never told anyone and you don't want to return the favour?'

'It's not about returning *favours*.' Irritation in her voice. 'Why is everything—?'

'What's your secret, Olivia?' He rolled her over so she was beneath him. Held her face between his hands so she had nowhere else to look but at him. 'Because I know you have one. I see it in your eyes. I hear it when you speak.'

Those eyes glittered with unshed tears. 'Make love to me, Jett.'

No words, just sighs and murmurs and whispers in the deepening twilight. They made love as if they hadn't had enough. As if they'd never get enough.

Make love to me, Jett. Her emotional plea echoed in the darkness for hours afterwards and it occurred to him as they lay in each other's arms that with Olivia, it wasn't just sex. It was deeper than pleasure. A closeness he'd never allowed himself to feel. It was a connection of more than mere body parts fitting together and it was unique, like her.

And *that* was the difference. He'd had sex with countless women but he'd never made love with anyone before.

CHAPTER FOURTEEN

THE NEXT MORNING they *eventually* got around to discussing their fundraising event.

'We can't have it till Brie comes back,' Olivia said, tapping her pen on the table.

Jett tipped back on his chair, studying the note pad in front of him. 'So three weeks?'

'Yes. It'll give us time to set it up.'

'So which idea are we going with?' he asked. As if he didn't know her mind was already made up.

By the end of the following day their plans were taking shape. Jett had taken her suggestion for a glitzy overnight dinner cruise in Hobart in his stride. It was a fitting way to honour her mother—yachting was in their blood, after all. He'd been assured this luxury cruising yacht was nothing like *Chasing Dawn* and they'd be on the calmer waters of the Derwent River, rather than on the high seas. They were to spend the night aboard. How could he refuse?

And all thanks to a multimillionaire oil magnate from Sydney with whom Olivia had made contact on Christmas Eve. Joe McPherson had listened to her story. His first wife had died of cancer and he was happy to make the trip south before he and his new wife set sail for Hawaii. The date had been set.

She arranged an online auction within the yacht clubs,

with the top five bidders and their partners at the end of one week to be the successful candidates. 'I know that's not many but it's a quality night and these people are seriously loaded. They'll also spread the word.'

'Whatever you want, it's your call.'

'It's about networking,' she told Jett. 'They knew Mum so it follows that they want to help Snowflake and will bid high. We don't need a crowd, we just need classy.'

Jett would be in charge of the menu and catering and would oversee the kitchen—*ahem*—galley. He'd hit on a few chefs he'd worked with who were prepared to work the evening at no cost and in return Jett would pay for their flights and upmarket overnight hotel accommodation.

By the end of the week they had their successful bidders with twice the amount they'd hoped for promised. Jett took Olivia to one of Hobart's fine dining restaurants at a popular art hotel on the waterfront to celebrate.

When Olivia thought she heard her phone buzzing a couple of nights later, she ignored it, burrowing deeper beneath the sheets and snuggling into the warm body behind her. She was exhausted, sleep-deprived—in the best way—and then there was that delicious man lying buck naked against her back. Nothing and no one was going to tempt her to leave her bed until at least lunch time. Maybe not even then.

An indeterminate while later she woke to the sound of her back door opening and footsteps crossing the kitchen tiles.

She shot upright, dragging the sheet to her chin, just in time to see Brie poke her head in her bedroom door. 'Hi ya, sleepy-head. Oops…' Her friend's eyes rounded in surprise and she looked away from the dark head on the pillow beside her. 'Sorry,' she whispered, backing up. 'I'll just disappear—'

Swinging her legs off the bed, Olivia glanced at Jett, oblivious to the world. 'The kitchen. Coffee. Go.'

'Sorry, Liv, I used my key when I couldn't get hold of you at the airport,' she said when they were both in the kitchen. 'I got a bit worried. But I can see everything's fine.' She lowered her voice. 'Who is that and where do I get one?'

Olivia couldn't help the smile that almost burst from her lips. 'You don't recognise him?'

'I only saw a broad outline and a nice firm slab of bronzed back and dark hair and—' Her eyes widened again. 'You've stolen my brother?'

'Not stolen. Borrowed.'

'You and Jett.' Her hands snuck up to her face to smother a grin. 'I thought he was going to Cradle Mountain?'

'He liked the view here better.'

'I want to hear everything. Or maybe not; he is my brother after all.'

'After coffee.' Olivia laughed. Hard to imagine they'd been lovers for a couple of weeks already. 'I'm starved—we didn't get around to dinner last night. It's become a bit of a habit I have to admit, which is a shame since his talents extend to the kitchen… But this one's my handiwork.' Olivia pointed at the slow cooker. 'Help yourself.'

'You *cooked*? *You*? For a *chef*? And not just any chef—'

'He bought me a cooker the other day. What else could I do? I won't tell you what happened with the salmon mousse when I tried to use the new food processor.'

'Ooh,' Brie murmured delightedly. 'You naughty girl.' She walked to the coffee machine and switched it on.

'No. No, it was nothing like that.' But Olivia's cheeks burned and she climbed onto a stool at the breakfast bar. 'Stay for lunch?'

They caught up on news over coffee. New Year's Eve, the break-in, Brie's holiday, the fundraiser plans. The reno-

ANNE OLIVER 161

vations and retreat. By the time they paused for breath they
were prepping salad for lunch.

'Hey.' The Voice. Deep, husky, morning-after voice.

They turned as one. 'Jett. Hi.' Brie set down the cucumber she was slicing and crossed the room to peck his cheek.
'This is a nice surprise.'

'What is?' he asked, feigning innocence as he touched his
lips to her brow while his eyes twinkled mischief at Olivia
over his sister's head.

Brie punched his arm. 'You, you idiot. And don't you look
relaxed? I like seeing Livvie pink-cheeked and happy too.'

While they all caught up, Olivia made a salad dressing
and thought how it could be—the three of them bound by
friendship, love and family. But he wasn't called the Jettsetter Chef for nothing. He was always off on some new
culinary adventure on the other side of the world. He was
helping out now but give him a couple of months in Tasmania to write his books and he'd be gone again.

She was darn well going to make the most of him while
he was here.

Over the next couple of weeks, funds for the dinner cruise
and late donations from the race rolled in. When Brie didn't
have clients, she came by to help with writing up job and
person specs for the new staff they'd need and to chat over
a wine or share a professionally cooked meal with them.

In addition to Brie's beauty therapy skills and Olivia's
business and natural therapy qualifications, they needed a
fitness instructor, a grounds-person, a therapeutic chef with
an enthusiasm for organics and raw food nutrition. A quali-
fied accountant on the books. Building contractors. More.

Jett enjoyed the freedom of working his own hours. Getting down and dirty in the garden. He experimented with
recipes in Olivia's kitchen and gave her some lessons in the

basics. Meanwhile he took inspiration from Tasmania's pure air and magnificent surroundings.

Every night he took a different kind of inspiration from the special woman he shared a bed with. Neither tried to define what they had or how long it might last. He pushed it to the back of his mind.

In the middle of the night when those thoughts and questions refused to stay away, he wrote. Within the week he'd finished a draft of a book that took his writing in a new direction. Its working title was *The Bare Ingredients: For Lovers of Food*. The Blue-Mint-Lagoon-cocktail-in-the-shower recipe featured front and centre. He was also working on other themes that Olivia had helped him come up with over hot chocolate when neither of them could sleep. She loved his idea of *Hot Tarts and Sexy Sauces* while the profits from her more demure suggestion of *Sugar and Spice and All Things Nice* would go into Snowflake's account.

They'd tried out some of his new sexy food ideas in the kitchen; he couldn't wait to try out more sensual food ideas—in the bedroom.

After the charity dinner cruise.

Before he left town.

He reminded himself he loved his unpredictable jet-setting life. New cities, new sights, new people. Freedom. No one to be accountable to. No reason to stick around.

Until now.

He frowned. *Now* his solo writing retreat and jet-loving lifestyle didn't excite him nearly as much as it had. Because now maybe he did have a reason to stay awhile—longer, even. He needed to be sure Olivia felt the same way.

She wasn't only his lover and confidante and friend. By her own words and actions, Olivia had taught him compassion and empathy. More, she'd made him reflect on his life and some of his decisions. She'd turned a cynical, commitment-phobic, self-centred guy into a better man.

A man who might even take a risk and consider something more...permanent.

He wanted to be with her, simple as that. Which meant putting his travel plans on hold indefinitely. For the first time in his life he wanted to build something that lasted.

And for the first time in his life if it didn't work out, it mattered.

Olivia snuck in a quick tour of *A King's Ransom* before their guests were due to board. The experienced crew remained aboard to sail the magnificent yacht, which dwarfed the marina with its sleek white lines, but the owner and his wife were staying ashore, enjoying a night at one of Hobart's top hotels.

Which left the captain's quarters—a stunning suite of several rooms—free for the two highest-bidding couples. She and Jett, Brie and her partner for the evening were bunking in the crew quarters, leaving the three staterooms for the remaining couples.

She checked her reflection on her way through one of the staterooms. Since she'd not had time to buy a new dress, Jett had organised Tyler to send her something a couple of days ago. A figure-hugging silver-grey halter neck with a thigh-high split. A flattering counterfoil for her sea-green eyes and auburn hair.

'Perfect.'

She glanced up at the familiar voice; her eyes flicked to Jett, who'd snuck up behind her. She'd never seen him in his chef's whites and her female hormones sighed. Her gaze gobbled him up as it drifted lower to admire a pair of black-and-white cargo pants. 'And you look sexy enough to eat.'

He moved in behind her, lowered his chin to the sensitive spot between neck and shoulder. 'Later,' he promised, a sinful glint in his eye.

She laughed. 'We're sharing space with two others tonight.'

'There's always tomorrow night.'

That glint changed from lightly teasing to something darker, deeper. It made her heart skip a beat then falter, and her humour faded. Maybe it was a trick of the light because he knew, like her, that there wouldn't always be a tomorrow night. Didn't he?

They'd not talked about the future; it was a tacit understanding that he'd move on, she'd stay in Tasmania. And that was how she wanted it. People were counting on her. Her career was mapped out for her. Her life—whatever happened—was here.

'I've been thinking about that chef's position for the retreat,' he murmured, his warm breath whispering over her shoulder.

Dread chilled her blood. No way could she allow Jett to see her deal with the imminent decisions she'd have to confront. To endure his pitying look if she chose a double mastectomy. He was making it impossible to ignore what she was trying so desperately to forget.

She flicked him a too-bright smile in the mirror. 'I wouldn't wait if I was you. It'll be months before the retreat's up and running. Your plan's always been to move on.' She switched topics, fingering the gown's fabric. Silky, smooth, sleek. 'Tyler's amazing. This is beautiful.'

'Not as beautiful as the woman it was made for.' His hands moved to her waist, down over her hips then they slid slowly up, cupping her breasts, his gaze following his movements in the mirror.

She smiled back, searching his eyes, hoping, *hoping* to

see the return of that flirty glint she'd seen a moment ago. Reminding her that they were just temporary.

'Your retreat may be a reality sooner than you think,' he said, then suddenly he was sliding a fine-spun rose-gold chain around her neck. Suspended from the chain was a small filigree snowflake the size of a fingernail sparkling with tiny pink stones.

Diamonds? Lord, she hoped not, but what else sparkled so brilliantly? Her heart skipped another beat as trembling fingers reached up to touch. 'Jett, I—'

'Good luck tonight,' he whispered, and was suddenly gone. As if he'd been about to say more but had changed his mind.

She stood a moment, staring at the gift in the mirror, unsure what to make of his words and the gesture. They'd been lovers such a short time. They'd made no secret of not wanting reminders so why had he given her something so expensive? So personal? So *memorable*?

He knew how upset she'd been about her stolen jewellery. That must be his reason. His words and actions tonight confused her.

'You okay, Livvie?' Brie asked from the doorway.

'Of course. I'm fine. Why wouldn't I be?' She pasted on a smile and admired Brie's backless midnight-blue dress. 'You look sensational. What's your date's name again?'

'So do you, and it's Theo. Liv...' She came right in and sat on the bed. 'You and Jett...it's getting serious between you two.'

'No.' Olivia fingered the necklace, avoided looking at her friend. 'It's just a fun ride and we're both enjoying it.'

'Can't you at least talk with Jett—?'

'No.' Shaking her head, she glared at Brie in the mirror. 'Promise me you won't either.'

Brie sighed. 'Okay, Liv. For now.'

'I want to live my life like everyone else. The way you do. Enjoy a fun no-strings romance with a nice guy. Until it's time to say goodbye.' Grabbing Brie's hand, she tugged her towards the door. 'It's going to be a fabulous night. You work one end of the room, I'll work the other.'

Olivia forced herself to cast doubts and questions aside and get on with the task of entertaining. The yacht was soon swamped with voices, movement and colour as the glitterati arrived, dripping in jewels and high-end fashion. The evocative sounds of flute and violin drifted from the classical music duo on deck. Expensive perfume mingled with the aroma of canapés being prepared in the galley. Wait staff circulated with drinks.

The water reflected a sliver of golden moon in a violet sky and they were about to set sail on a floating palace. But Olivia didn't have time to enjoy the view, ensuring guests were comfortable on the awesome outside entertainment area strewn with candles in coloured glass pots.

'And the big question on every woman's lips is will the Jettsetter Chef be making an appearance?'

'After dinner,' Olivia told a female reporter, almost wishing she hadn't invited the media to attend the guests' arrival and to interview her. 'But you won't be here then.' She smiled sweetly because she knew the woman would be disappointed, and slid a glass of sparkling water from a passing waiter's tray. 'But Pink Snowflake—'

'There he is!' The woman swivelled on her heel, sidestepped Olivia and made a beeline towards him, her heels clicking over polished wood.

Olivia turned, surprised to see his unexpected appearance, and their gazes clashed across the deck. Without thought, her hand reached up to touch the chain at her neck. He noticed her small movement, and a slow smile spread over his face. Then the reporter blocked her view and Olivia turned away, her mind whirling, only to be confronted with another journalist who'd obviously witnessed the intimate exchange.

She studied Olivia's face, her eyes alive with speculation. 'And will we be seeing more of the pair of you out and about?' Her ID showed she was from the women's magazine that was donating a hefty sum for an interview.

'Whatever do you mean?' Olivia said. 'We're not here to speculate on gossip. We're here to talk about the Pink Snowflake Foundation—that's the important message for tonight...'

At last the media left and the magnificent cruise yacht sailed out of the marina, the lights of the CBD and the casino glittering from the shore.

The main course was a choice of liquorice-braised leg of lamb with Jerusalem artichoke and caramelised onion purée or roasted pork shoulder with swede, pickled rhubarb purée, sage and apple dressing, all served at a massive oak dining table.

Olivia found herself sitting opposite James Harrison, owner of a string of successful Sydney nightclubs. Mid-forties, attractive. A playboy edge about that smile even with his partner, Sue, right alongside. Sue paid him no attention, more interested in talking to Sandra Hemsworth to her right.

'I hope you'll drop by the club when you're in Sydney.' He twinkled those playboy blue eyes at her and slid a business card across the table. 'Contact me and I'll make sure I'm there.'

Not *we*, she noted. 'Um...I don't know when I'll get to Sydney, James, with so much going on at the moment.'

'Jim.'

'Jim.' She glanced at Sue, who'd turned and was watching them with a smile on her lips.

'I'm his sister,' she said. 'In case you were wondering.'

'Oh.' Olivia laughed, but suddenly a new kind of tension gripped her. Because James—Jim—was definitely interested. And Olivia definitely was not. She snatched up her wine glass. 'So does being in business with family members work for you...?'

For the remainder of the meal she managed to keep the conversation focused on their nightclubs and her charity. And yachting of course. She slipped *Chasing Dawn* into the conversation in the hope that James or Sue or anyone in on the conversation might know of an interested buyer. Someone who'd love the little yacht the way she did.

A selection of desserts and coffee was served in the entertainment area where the only formalities for the evening took place. Jett and his assistant chefs made an appearance so the guests could acknowledge their efforts.

He and his mates accepted the applause with good cheer. Olivia made a short speech thanking everyone for their amazing support and wishing them a pleasant evening. Finally, Brie spoke about Snowflake on Olivia's behalf.

When it was over with guests free to choose whatever they wanted to do until breakfast, Olivia escaped to a dark corner of the deck alone. She hugged her arms in the coolish briny air. Jett's work for the night was done. He'd be looking for her any minute and she wished she knew what she was going to say.

How was she going to respond if he mentioned the chef's position again? Because then she'd have to put him—

'It's a pretty night.'

She glanced at the masculine voice beside her and wished herself elsewhere. But she lifted her voice, smiled to match. 'James.'

'Jim.'

'Jim. Yes, it is.'

'So...you're serious about selling *Chasing Dawn*?'

She turned to him, found him not as attractive as she'd first thought. But then she'd never find another man as attractive as Jett. 'She's a seventy-year-old wooden-hulled boat. I need someone who'll love her like I do, scars and all.'

'Whatever your asking price, I'll double it.'

She hesitated. Silly to be sentimental over a pile of old wood. She could do so much more good with cold hard cash. And she'd still have the misty, water-coloured memories of her and her mum exploring the bays and inlets around Tassie.

But why did a man like James Harrison, a previous winner of the Australian Bluewater Classic with his ginormous maxi yacht, want an itty-bitty scrap of a boat like *Chasing Dawn*?

Jett caught sight of Olivia on the deck and was about to head over when he realised someone was going to beat him to it. The same guy who'd been eying her off when Jett and his fellow chefs had joined the guests for coffee. And a feeling he'd never known had gripped him hard, held him so tightly he'd barely been able to breathe.

It was still there, like an iron fist clamped around his gut. *Jealousy.* His chef's jacket was suddenly strangling him and he flicked open the top button. He could hear their conversation on the still evening air. Not only was the man eying his woman off, he wanted her boat.

She was still considering selling *Chasing Dawn*? *No way.* She loved that boat too much. Jett was by her side in a few quick strides. 'Mate, you're too late.'

'What?' Olivia's hand flew to her chest, her eyes widened in fright. 'Jett, where did you spring from? And what do you mean?'

'Sorry, babe, didn't mean to scare you.' He stuck out his hand to the guy. 'Jett Davies.'

'Jim.' The man shook Jett's hand. 'Nice meal tonight, Jett.'

Nice. Right. Spectacular, more like. Jett's lip curled but he managed to transform it into a rough resemblance of a grin. 'Yeah, as I was saying—sorry, Jim, she's promised it to me.' He tugged her to his side. 'Right, skipper?'

Jim frowned, looked to her for confirmation then frowned again, his gaze flicking between the two of them. 'Is that right, Olivia?'

She slipped out of Jett's hold and stepped away from both of them, hands raised in front of her breasts in a defensive gesture. 'I…um. I'm still deciding.'

And Jett had a bad feeling it wasn't only the boat she was talking about. The first trickle of real unease rose up his throat. 'Olivia, I—'

Her eyes widened, then turned hard and uncompromising. 'If you'll both excuse me…' She turned on one stilettoed heel and walked away, leaving the two of them standing on the deck throwing metaphoric daggers at each other.

Dammit. He shrugged at Jim. 'That's Olivia for you. She's been under stress to get this night happening,' he explained. 'I'll make sure she rests when we get home tomorrow.' He saw he'd got his message across and walked away whistling.

But he knew he'd stepped over a line with Olivia. She demanded her independence and he'd not respected her decision to sell her boat if that was what she chose to do.

He needed to fix his wrong. But how? He knew from experience she took that kind of behaviour very much to heart.

CHAPTER FIFTEEN

OLIVIA DIDN'T FIND it hard to avoid Jett for the rest of the evening because he seemed to be staying well away. She didn't see him on the deck again when she walked there with a few guests to watch the yacht pass beneath the Tasman Bridge. Nor in the entertainment area when nightcaps were served. But it played on her nerves until they were stretched to breaking point as they tied up at the marina for the night. At last the final couple said goodnight and headed to bed and she breathed a sigh of relief.

He was waiting for her in the crew's quarters, lying on a bunk, hands behind his head. The moment he caught sight of her, he tensed and pushed up, dominating the cramped space with his size. 'You all right?'

No. 'What were you thinking overriding me that way? I do not need you or anyone else telling me what to do. It's my life, my choices.' She didn't want to know his reasons. For any of it. 'I don't want an argument, I—'

'Which is why I'm leaving.' He reached for his bag, hefted it over his shoulder.

'Leaving?' Olivia's stomach dropped like a stone. 'I just meant—'

'It's okay, skipper.' He smiled but it wasn't the brash, confident Jett she knew and respected.

And loved.

'I know you don't want a scene,' he continued as he side-stepped past her in the narrow space between bunks on his way out. 'And this isn't the time or place.' He dropped a feather-soft kiss on her brow. 'The evening was a well-deserved success for Pink Snowflake. Congratulations.'

She wanted to put her arms around his neck and tell him she hadn't meant to jump all over him like that the moment she'd seen him, like some nag. She wanted to say sorry and ask him to stay but she knew he was right, there was too much unresolved tension between them, and nothing could be resolved here tonight within earshot of others. 'I couldn't have done it without you,' she said to his back.

He turned at the doorway and smiled that tired kind of smile again. 'Sure you could.'

She barely slept. The night seemed interminable. She blamed the narrow bunk but she missed the feel of Jett's warm body beside hers. His last words echoed in her head with the far-away look in his eyes. *Sure you could.*

What had he meant by that? Was it a genuine belief in her abilities or was it her cue to go it alone? The truth was she didn't *want* to do it alone. Not any more. She'd miss his confidence and his culinary skills, the way he made her laugh and forget her problems. She'd miss their robust discussions.

She'd miss *him*.

The more she thought about the evening, the more she knew he was letting her down gently. He was leaving. The necklace was a parting gift. His talk about the chef's position and the retreat being a reality sooner than she thought… he meant the foundation was growing quicker than they'd expected, that was all. That he wouldn't be needed; it was time to move on.

And she was ready. Her heart was breaking but she was

prepared. She didn't want to do it alone, but she could. She would.

It was almost a relief to get up and check that everything had been cleared away to her satisfaction and check that the informal breakfast had been set out before the catering crew had left.

She'd arranged to meet the owner and his wife, Joe and Tessa McPherson, for coffee at nine a.m. in the hotel, so she wasn't expecting them to board while she was still break-fasting with the guests at seven-thirty.

'Joe, Tessa. Good morning to you.' She rose to meet the well-dressed couple. 'Did I get the times wrong?'

'No.' Joe beamed at her, his ruddy complexion glowing. 'Tess and I wanted to make sure to catch you before you all left. We have a little something for you.' He drew a piece of paper from the inside pocket of his navy jacket. 'We be-lieve in the Pink Snowflake Foundation and what you're doing. You blew me away with your enthusiasm on Christ-mas Eve—Tess'll tell you I kept her awake half the night talking about it. I love a good cause.'

Olivia smiled. 'So do I. Sorry, Tessa, if I was the reason for you not getting a good night's sleep.'

'No problem.' Tessa smiled back, her carefully styled blonde hair glinting in the morning sun that slanted through the windows.

Joe exchanged a fond glance with his younger wife. 'She and I had a talk,' he went on. 'We loved the philosophy be-hind the name—individuals together making a difference. We'd like to be a part of your retreat. And we'd like to see it built in the next six months rather than the next fifty years, so we're giving you a head start.' He handed Olivia a cheque made out to the Pink Snowflake Foundation.

Enthusiastic applause followed and then Brie was hug-ging her and looking over her shoulder. 'Wow.'

'Oh, my.' Olivia stared at the six-figure amount for a long moment as a numb feeling of disbelief and excitement and gratitude crept up her body. 'I don't know how to thank you.' She paused, suddenly knowing the very best way. 'Yes, I do. We'll name it the McPherson Retreat.'

Sweat poured down his back, into his eyes. Jett yanked off his T-shirt, tossed it across a stunted bush and jammed the spade into the hard-packed earth again. Again. He wanted the distraction of heat, the heavy load, the hard work.

'Jett...'

He looked up, slightly dazed in the heat, realising he'd heard his name more than once. Olivia was watching him—had been for some time by the look in her eyes. Her apricot-cucumber fragrance rose to greet him as she held out a glass.

'Here, drink.'

'Thanks.' He swallowed it down in a few greedy gulps. 'How long have you been back?' He picked up the spade again.

'Long enough to see that you're going to do serious damage if you don't slow down.' All calmness, she took the spade from his hands, tossed it down. 'No more. You worked all yesterday, then last night. It's hot out here and heatstroke's not funny.'

'Last night was worth it, right?' With nothing in his hands, he struggled to channel his energy—he was a volcano about to erupt. 'You were sensational.'

'It was worth it, but it wasn't only me. The menu was amazing. You and your staff were fantastic. And you haven't heard the good news. The McPhersons donated enough money to build the extension. We'll have it up in months.'

'That *is* good news. But I let you down. I shouldn't have left you to do breakfast on your own.' He ran a grime-smeared hand through his hair, annoyed at her calm demeanour. He wanted her angry. He wanted fire; he wanted that edge, that connection, not this calm woman with no bite.

'Not a problem. Everything was already there, we only had to—'

'What were you thinking?' he shouted, switching to what was *really* pissing him off. '*Chasing Dawn*'s not for sale.'

Her eyes widened in surprise and her voice rose. 'Says who? *You?*'

Better. 'Yeah. Me. Not to him.'

'Jim? Why not?'

'I didn't like the cut of his jacket. Hell, I didn't like the man's name, the man's aftershave, the man's— He was coming on to you—didn't you realise that?'

'And what if he was?' she demanded, white-lipped now, eyes spitting fire. 'I wasn't reciprocating—or didn't you notice? But you and me—we're temporary. We've always known that. Sooner or later you're leaving.'

'Hang on—'

She waved him away. 'You said I could do it on my own.'

He frowned. '*What? When?*'

'Last night. When you left me standing there with your parting gift around my neck. I said I couldn't have done it without you and you said—'

Sure you could...

She'd misinterpreted his words. Frustration zigged up his spine and he scratched the back of his neck.

'Olivia...sweetheart... That's not what I meant.' He saw confusion cloud her eyes and took a step forward, hands raised. 'I meant you are the most capable woman I've ever met—not that I wanted you to go it alone. If I didn't make it clear enough, I'm sorry.'

She shook her head once, and seemed to shrink in on herself, as if she didn't want to hear.

'And *parting gift?*' Unease was crawling over his skin

like ants. 'It was a thank-you-I-think-you're-pretty-damn-special gift. You didn't pick up on that?'

'I...don't know... A man's never given me anything so... intimate or expensive.'

'And you're the first woman I've ever bought jewellery for,' he told her as he approached, partially reassured by her sudden stillness. 'The *only* woman I'll *ever* buy jewellery for.'

'Jett. I think you should...'

When he reached her, he gripped her fine-boned shoulders and poured his heart and soul into the bottomless well of her gaze. 'You made me look further than skin deep. I love how you make me laugh. I love how we argue and make up. How you turn good into bad. How you make me accountable for the words that come out of my mouth.'

His grip tightened because for the first time in his life he was laying everything he had on the line and she wasn't responding—at least not the way he'd hoped. 'I've been a drifter all my life. You're the only woman who's ever made me want to stick around. To take a risk on us. I want to stay here with you and be a part of your dream.

'I'm applying for the chef's position, even if it's two years down the track, because I'll still be here in twenty years, working alongside you to make that dream reality.' He brushed the damp hair back from her brow, struggling not to panic.

'If it's still not clear, I'll put it in a few simple words. Commitment. For ever. Family. I want to see you in a rocking chair nursing our first child at your breast. I want to see you in that same rocking chair when we celebrate our sixtieth wedding anniversary surrounded by grandch—'

'And if I don't have those breasts you so admire, *what then*?' The words spilled from Olivia's tongue before she could censor them. Pain at the injustice of it all lanced through her heart. *Why her?* Why was fate denying her what she wanted most?

His brow creased. 'What do you mean?'

'Kids? Marriage?' Her eyes stung with tears she *refused* to allow. 'What's wrong with what we have now?'

The power of those turbulent dark eyes was a physical force. 'It's not enough now. I want more. I found a sister, then I found her best friend and I've decided family's a pretty good deal.'

'No.' She shook her head, her heart breaking. 'I have my life planned out and it doesn't include family. Jett Davies, Jettsetter Chef extraordinaire, globe-trotter and the brother of my best friend, Brie's your family and she loves you.'

'I know who I am,' he snapped, 'and I know who you are. *You're the woman I love.*'

Love. The word reverberated in the air between them and their incredulous gazes clashed. As if Jett was as surprised— and devastated—as she.

There was a cruel fist squeezing her heart, crushing it to dust. She shook her head. 'No. That's not what we agreed on.'

His fingers tightened on her arms and he pulled her up, so her feet dangled off the ground, so all she could see was him. Desperation. Despair. Anguish. 'So tell me to go away. Tell me you don't want me in your life.'

'It's not that simple.'

'Yes, Olivia. It is.' He loosened his hold so suddenly that she stumbled backwards. She saw the tormented twist of his mouth, the desolation in his eyes and knew she'd hurt him the way he'd been hurt so many times in his past.

'Please, Jett, it was never my intention to hurt you. You have to believe that.'

'I'll be out of your way in thirty minutes,' he said, defeat reducing his voice to not much more than a harsh under-tone. 'Until then, I'd appreciate it if you stay out of mine.'

He turned away. He was doing as he'd said. Walking out of her life. For ever.

'Wait.' *One more look.* Her hand fisted against her breast-bone. He stopped but didn't turn around. 'I need to tell you something before you leave.'

A bare nod was his only response. She couldn't see his expression but his posture was so tense she wondered that he didn't snap in two. 'Thank you. For everything.'

There must have been something in the way she spoke because he swung back to her. Dark eyes probed hers for a long moment. 'Are you ill? Is that it?'

A glimmer of a smile touched her lips that he'd got it so right. 'Not that I know of.' Yet.

His shoulders relaxed marginally, but his expression re-mained grim, his jaw rigid. 'Anything else?'

She shook her head. *Except that I love you and maybe you'll understand why I made this choice one day.*

He shook his head and resumed walking.

Olivia kept out of his way. She sat on the balcony, star-ing dry-eyed but sightless in the direction of the Derwent River until she heard Jett's rental car leave. Then she got busy. She stripped her bed, changed towels. *No reminders.*

When Brie's happy tune jingled on her phone an hour later, she switched it off and buried it at the bottom of her handbag and kept working.

She'd call Brie tomorrow. Explain. Make her understand. Then she'd take out *Chasing Dawn* and maybe spend the night on the water under the stars, the way she and her mum used to do. As she'd done the night after she'd died.

Her ruthless frenzy didn't abate until mid-afternoon. Until she found his favourite jumper tucked down the edge of the sofa amongst the cushions. The pain knocked the breath from her lungs and she sank to the floor, remembering how the soft cashmere had felt when he'd held her against his chest only a couple of chilly evenings ago. She buried her nose in its folds and the floodgates opened.

Jett parked his rental halfway up Olivia's driveway, cut the engine. From here he could see her car, so he knew she was still inside. And if she had any ideas about leaving she'd have to detour around him. Make that *try* to detour around him because neither of them were going anywhere until she told him the whole story.

He'd gone to the one person he could turn to. Breanna had hugged him then ordered him to sit down and share the pot of rosehip tea she'd just made. And while he drank, she'd talked.

'I promised not to tell,' she said, 'but have you wondered why Livvie's so driven? Why everything's got to be done yesterday? How she can study, work, run a charity and plan a retreat?

'Why she'd push you away when her eyes tell you something entirely different?'

And in his mind's eye he saw her New Year's Day when they'd made love on the dining table in the hotel. Radiating such a vibrant energy it was *as if she was trying to live an entire life in those few crazy moments.*

He had his answer.

And the bottom plunged out of his world. 'She's dying.'

'No.'

Breanna smiled but her eyes were different and he knew he had part of it right. 'Then I don't get it. Her mother, her family history...'

'Go back. Make her talk to you.'

* * *

Olivia didn't hear him come in, didn't see him until he sat down on the floor beside her and a half-empty box of tissues. 'Olivia.'

His voice—calm seas. But she got a glimpse of dark, stormy ocean in his eyes before she looked down at her hands twisting in his jumper. 'How did you get in?'

'Breanna gave me her key.'

She swiped at her wet cheeks. 'She told you. She promised—'

'She didn't tell me,' he said quietly. 'She gave me her key so *you* could tell me.'

She closed her eyes. 'Why have you come back?'

'Some treasures are worth sticking around for—so are some troubles. And sometimes they're one and the same.'

'Not this trouble.'

'Let me make my own decisions about the kind of trouble I want to get involved in. And it *is* my concern, whether you like it or not. Because I love you. I'll always love you. Whatever happens.'

Tears filled her eyes and spilled over in her heart. 'You shouldn't.'

He shifted closer, so that their shoulders touched. 'Just answer me this. Do you love me back?'

She could no longer deny her heart. 'I do. I love you.' She sighed, drained to the bottom of her soul. 'But it doesn't matter.'

'You're wrong. It matters. Look at me.' Tucking a finger beneath her chin, he turned her towards him so she could see the truth in his eyes. He brushed her hair off her face and said, 'It matters more than my next breath. You've trusted me before—do you still trust me?'

'Yes…but this is dif—'

He pressed a finger to her lips. 'No buts. I promise I'll

still be here in the morning. And next week. Next year. For however long you love me.'

'I'll always love you, Jett. But I don't know how long that "always" might be.' She turned away. 'I'm not a long term kind of girl.'

'You're *my* kind of girl. Who knows how long any of us have? We could be swept away in a flood tomorrow. Talk to me, sweetheart.'

'I'm waiting on some test results.'

'And…?'

'And…the women in my family all carried the same gene mutation. The test will show whether I do too.' She bit her lip. 'I'm scared.'

'It's okay to be scared.' He wrapped his arms around her, enfolding her in a comforting blanket of warmth and security. 'I'm scared too. But we're going to deal with it together. You're tough, resilient, formidable even. We'll get through this even though you tried to spare me and make a difference to others facing the same illness. Which also makes you the most unselfish person I've ever met.'

She shook her head. 'Not so unselfish. I've crammed my life with work and fundraising as a distraction as much as anything else.'

'You could have distracted yourself in plenty of other, more self-satisfying ways.'

'I did. That's why I messed around with you.'

'A very good decision.'

His arms tightened and she leaned against his chest and said, 'When I knew I was falling for you…' she took a stuttering breath '…I tried to keep it casual. I pushed you away because maybe you'd meet someone who wanted long term, with…kids and everything.'

'Who are you to make that decision for me? I deserve to make that choice myself. I thought we agreed on making our own choices a while ago.'

'I guess I didn't see it clearly in this instance.'

'What are the chances of a positive result?' he murmured into her hair.

'High.'

He kissed the side of her face. 'Better to know the worst now than to have it nagging at the back of our minds. Whichever way it goes, we can make plans. Together.'

'But what about kids? Family?'

'Without you? Not a chance.'

He was risking his own happiness, his shot at a family. He'd stay with her for however long or short that might be. Relief and happiness were washing over her like waves. 'I didn't realise how much I needed you until you walked away.'

'No one's ever needed me before. Do you know how that feels?'

'Wonderful. Special. Amazing. Because now I know you need me too. I was wrong to deny you that chance.'

'So get it into your head, I'm with you all the way. But I'm confident it's going to be good news.'

'Good news. But if it's not, there are important decisions to make, like whether to have surgery or—'

'Not now.' He stopped her with a finger to her lips.

'If you'd gone...'

'I wasn't going anywhere without answers. I don't give up that easily. But when I realised what was going on I didn't know the best way to get through to you. Lucky I have Breanna.'

She wrapped her fingers around his and squeezed. 'Lucky. Families are the best.'

* * *

'Satellite number two, right on time, skipper.' Jett pointed to the night sky a couple of weeks later. They'd taken *Chasing Dawn* out for a short sail while the weather was calm, and were lying side by side on the deck and watching the stars. Only their fingers touched and for Jett it was the most spiritual feeling he'd ever known. The two of them alone beneath the wonders of the universe.

'Well spotted.' His stargazer, satellite-spotter sailor lover tapped the back of his hand with a fingernail.

'I read up on how to interpret the test results,' he said, still tracking the satellite's slow steady arc across the sky. 'If your results are negative for a known family mutation, your risk of developing cancer is no greater than mine. It's called a true negative.' He turned his head to look at her. 'But I guess you already know that.'

'Yes.' She turned her head on the wooden deck and looked back at him, her eyes reflecting the star sparkle. 'We just have to wait.'

'There's something I don't want to wait for,' he said, and raised himself up on one elbow. She looked so beautiful lying there, bathed in starlight, his pink snowflake charm winking at her throat. 'This is as good a place as any to ask you to marry me.'

Her eyes went round and wide. 'Marry you? But don't you want to wait until—?'

'Not another word.' His eyes narrowed.

'I only meant until the moon rises.' She cast her gaze to the growing shimmery glow on the eastern horizon, then smiled back at him. 'In ten minutes, give or take.'

'Okay.' He relaxed again and rolled towards her. 'I guess I can find something to do for ten minutes. Give or take.'

'Are you planning on getting *nautical* with me, Chef Davies?' she said, reaching for his belt.

'With a dash of piratical flavour,' he promised.

'Marriage...' Olivia tried out the word a short time later, feeling incredibly lazy and loose and loved, as they watched the first sliver of moon rise over the rugged coastline.

'Commitment. Now. No matter what happens we're in this together. And to prove it...'

He slid a ring onto the third finger of her left hand. A snowflake mounted on a rose-gold band to match the one around her neck. 'Oh, my. Pink diamonds. Again.' She grinned at him and caressed it with her other hand. 'It's perfect. Absolutely perfect. And it matches my necklace.'

'I doubt it's practical for everyday use but when I had the other one made, I decided I wanted this too.'

Laughing, she threw her arms around his neck. 'I love impractical. And I love you... Hang on—' Pulling back, she watched his expression while she replayed his words in her head. 'You had it made *when* exactly?'

He didn't reply but his trade-mark cocky grin spread over his face.

She grinned back. 'I do love a confident man.'

EPILOGUE

'BRIE'S LATE. I don't know why we didn't pick her up on the way.' Olivia tapped her fingers on the snowy cloth in one of Hobart's premier restaurants. Which drew her attention to her engagement ring glittering like a million dollars. She couldn't keep the grin from her lips. She'd spent a lot of time gazing at her left hand over the past couple of weeks, reminding herself that no matter what the future held, she'd not be alone.

That if the going got tough, Jett wasn't going anywhere.

Even though it made no difference to their plans, she and Jett had kept their upcoming nuptials a secret until Olivia had her test results in her hot little hand. Today's negative result meant she was no more at risk of cancer than anyone else in the community. And she couldn't wait to tell her best friend and future sister-in-law.

'Relax.' Jett poured chilled champagne into two glasses. 'Breanna's not famous for her time-keeping skills. She was meeting someone first.' His lips twitched. 'She texted me they were having car problems.'

'Oh? *Oh...*' Olivia nodded. That said it all.

She spotted Brie making her way between the tables a couple of glasses of wine and an entrée later.

'What are we celebrating?' Brie wasted no time asking

as she sat down and took the glass Jett held out to her. 'We did the engagement, so it has to be something else.'

'Two things, actually.' Olivia clasped her hands together in front of her mouth, unable to contain her joy a second more. 'I got my test results today. And it's negative.'

'Oh, Livvie!' Brie jumped up and came around the table to hug her. 'I'm so, so happy for you. For both of you.' She moved on to Jett and hugged him too. Finally, she leaned back, her gaze flitting between the pair of them. 'You said two things.'

Jett looked at Olivia and all the love and promises and future shone in his eyes. 'We're getting married in a week.'

'A week?' Brie squealed. 'My brother the fast worker.'

Olivia laughed. 'We want to be a family. And, my wonderful sister-in-law-to-be, that includes you. The ceremony's going to be on *Chasing Dawn* at sunset on Sunday and we want you and a friend to be our witnesses.'

'So romantic.' Brie nodded, a playful smile around her mouth. 'Count me in. Oh, wait up.' She whipped out her phone and began snapping photos. 'I want memories for that album of yours, starting now.'

Olivia met Jett's persuasive chocolate eyes and, as always, felt herself surrendering to his wicked sense of fun, to his easy friendship. To his love. And she knew they'd make a long and happy lifetime of memories. 'I think it's time we posed for a kissy photo to put on the front cover.'

Jett smiled and leaned down, stroking a strand of hair behind her ear and cradling her chin in his cupped palm. 'I reckon it is.'

* * * * *

A sneaky peek at next month...

MODERN tempted™

**FRESH, CONTEMPORARY ROMANCES TO TEMPT
ALL LOVERS OF GREAT STORIES**

My wish list for next month's titles...

In stores from 15th November 2013:

❏ The Most Expensive Night of Her Life
    — Amy Andrews

❏ The Reunion Lie — Lucy King

In stores from 6th December 2013:

❏ Too Much of a Good Thing? — Joss Wood

❏ Beware of the Boss — Leah Ashton

Available at WHSmith, Tesco, Asda, Eason, Amazon and Apple

Just can't wait?

*Visit us
Online*

You can buy our books online a month before
they hit the shops! **www.millsandboon.co.uk**

Special Offers

Every month we put together collections and longer reads written by your favourite authors.

Here are some of next month's highlights— and don't miss our fabulous discount online!

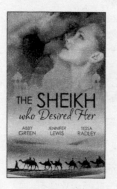

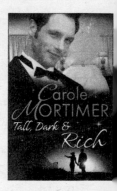

On sale 6th December **On sale 1st November** **On sale 6th December**

Save 20%
on all Special Releases

Wrap up warm this winter with Sarah Morgan...

Sleigh Bells in the Snow

Kayla Green loves business and hates Christmas.

So when Jackson O'Neil invites her to Snow Crystal Resort to discuss their business proposal... the last thing she's expecting is to stay for Christmas dinner. As the snowflakes continue to fall, will the woman who doesn't believe in the magic of Christmas finally fall under its spell...?

4th October

www.millsandboon.co.uk/sarahmorgan

/MB435

Come home this Christmas to Fiona Harper

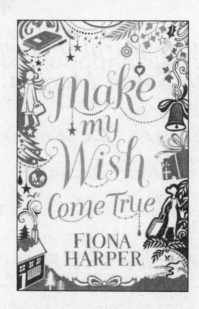

From the author of *Kiss Me Under the Mistletoe* comes a
Christmas tale of family and fun. Two sisters are ready
to swap their Christmases—the busy super-mum, Juliet,
getting the chance to escape it all on an exotic Christmas
getaway, whilst her glamorous work-obsessed sister,
Gemma, is plunged headfirst into the family Christmas
she always thought she'd hate.

www.millsandboon.co.uk